PATRICIA

AND

MALISE

by

Susanna Johnston

GIBSON SQUARE

This is a work of fiction, in which the events are entirely imaginary.
Any coincidence between living persons and named characters
in the novel is purely fortuitous.

This edition published by Gibson Square for the first time

UK Tel: +44 (0)20 7096 1100
US Tel: +1 646 216 9813

info@gibsonsquare.com
www.gibsonsquare.com

ISBN   9781783340880
eISBN   9781783341344

The moral right of Susanna Johnston to be identified as the author of this work has been asserted in accordance with the Copyright, Designs and Patents Act 1988.

Papers used by Gibson Square are natural, recyclable products made from wood grown in sustainable forests; inks used are vegetable based. Manufacturing conforms to ISO 14001, and is accredited to FSC and PEFC chain of custody schemes. Colour-printing is through a certified CarbonNeutral® company that offsets its CO2 emissions.

PATRICIA AND MALISE

1

The brothers, almost from birth, disapproved of smoking – long before it became fashionable to do so – although neither of them ever came within many miles of being fashionable.

Malise did strain at times to attain a worldly air but Christian never attempted it.

They were born, sons to a withered scion of a Scottish ducal family and his bible-believing wife who lived in an ancient farmhouse in a rural part of Hertfordshire.

In a Spartan nursery they were taught to redeem and to reform. When Malise was no more than four years old he, with the help of his mother and much attention to detail, mended the foot of an inherited rocking-horse that they were not allowed to ride or to play with on Sundays. As he patted putty into a front hoof, Malise frowned crossly at the wobbliness of his miniature spatula. His mother, Madeline, spoke quietly. 'Remember, Malise. A good workman never blames his tools.'

Madeline had a large flat face and two large flat plaits were pinned to the top of her head by pale hair pins. Very much later Malise remembered her words and, later still, congratulated himself on never having blamed his tool for anything.

Malise's mother often explained to him 'I chose your name, dear, upon learning that it's Gaelic origin came from the words 'Servant of Jesus.' She loved and rejoiced in the name although it unnerved her when the occasional visitor mispronounced it.

Christian needed no explanation for his given name.

Their father, older than his wife, was quiet and stately. He passed his time studying, in a wandering way, maps and atlases. A vast globe rotated on his desk but he had no desire to travel.

Although the farmhouse was rambling, the 'boys' were expected to share a bedroom. Two narrow wrought-iron beds stood on, as was also laid in the nursery and bathroom, beige linoleum floor covering. A solitary picture hung on one of the walls. It was a much reproduced coloured print of the shining figure of Jesus – with only the faintest suspicion of a cross in the background. Under it was written 'All Things Bright and Beautiful.'

Apart from this reproduction, the room was bare. A copy of the Bible lay beside each bed and on each hard pillow lived a Teddy bear. These Teddy bears remained with the boys until the end of each of their lives.

Malise was perfectly formed. He had blue eyes, fair curls, a strong body and classical features.

Christian, four years younger than his brother, was a poor replica. They were alike but Christian's hair grew lower over his brow. His cheeks were rough and ruddy and his movements clumsy. From the word go he had been unable to pronounce his r's which made it a tall order when it came to saying his name. He deified his brother who delighted in calling him 'Cwistian.' Nearly every day he made the small boy repeat, after him, the words 'I tripped up on the slippery road after the soft refreshing rain.'

By the time Christian was five, his brother nine, they read tracts, set out for them by their mother, and wrote down sayings to pin up on a cork board in the nursery. 'Neither a lender nor a borrower be' was the favoured one. Although money was not scarce in the family, it was extremely important that they learn the value of it and how it should never be spent unnecessarily, particularly on others.

Malise learnt and recited these dictums aloud.

Christian uttered little for fear of mockery.

Such was their life until one Wednesday, when the boys were ten and six respectively, their mother died in her sleep. She had been weakening for many months but the fact of her illness had never been mentioned in front of her sons.

In Madeline's dead hands she clasped one verse of her favourite hymn – written shakily as she struggled with a relief nib dipped into black ink and began –

In every condition, in sickness, in health
In poverty's vale or abounding in wealth ....

Some months earlier, when she knew her strength to be failing and with a small legacy of her own, she had commissioned a portrait of Malise to be painted. Every strand of his golden hair glistened on canvas. Whilst trying hard not to bracket this work of art with her own image of Christ, the enamoured mother hung it as an icon above her table.

Poor little Christian, unpainted, did nothing but worship his Adonis of a brother and sometimes, in secret, prayed before the picture as and when he was allowed to greet his mother in the mornings – before she lost herself in hours of prayer.

Neither boy was allowed to attend their mothers' funeral but watched the hearse from a dining-room window as it drove her slowly away, followed by their father on foot.

Soon after that they began to be incongruously playful together. It was Malise who, with scientific patience, showed Christian the way – as soon as the overhead light (the only one in the room) was switched off. The beds were hard and narrow so they used the floor. With no mother to hear them recite their prayers, there was little danger of interruption – since their father kept to his own forlorn quarters.

It started as a semi-game with Malise ordering a dazzled Christian (alive with joy that his brother wished to play with him) to lie on the floor.

'Now' the older one would say, 'Squeeze me as if I were a toothpaste tube. Start at the bottom, of course, as mother taught us to do with toothpaste.'

Malise taunted Christian as well as practicing antics on him and often chanted 'you are the stone that the builder rejected' as he conducted sexual experiments. After each session he would take Christian to the chilly bathroom for a wash. There he always pointed to one of the many maxims that covered walls throughout the house. 'Please remember, don't forget. Never leave the bathroom wet.'

Christian remained doting and admiring. Together they went, Malise first, of course, to a daily, local private school – fees were paid by the distant ducal trust.

A heavily built spinster neighbour called for them and ferried them to and fro. She had pity for the motherless boys and designs on their father.

The ritual seldom varied. Alyson, as the spinster was called, nearly always shouted out a loud 'cooeee' in the dark hall. 'I've left a little something on the kitchen table so that you and your Daddy can have a bit of a tuck in tonight.' Malise was squeamish and, even then, detested the way that Alyson spoke of their father as 'Daddy.' That was something that never changed even with the passing of many years.

2

By the time Malise, a prodigiously handsome thirteen year old, went off to public school, the boys had become accustomed to a step-mother – Alyson, the one to have driven them (and continued to do so in the case of Christian) to day school. She was flat footed, flat voiced and not at all interfering. Nonetheless she wanted to mother the boys and was not to be trusted where 'popping in' to say goodnight was concerned. In some ways this made their rituals more exciting and the expectation of one of her appearances heightened the intensity. She did once find them on the floor together but tip toed out of the room and closing the door quietly behind her, padded downstairs to tell her dozing husband 'It was refreshing, if naughty after lights out, to see them ragging and getting on so well together.'

All that ended when Alyson, accompanied by Christian – silent and stifled in the back seat – drove Malise and his trunk (Teddy bear packed) to the nearest station. Christian's life emptied as the train puffed away. Alyson made an attempt to kiss Malise goodbye but the plan misfired as the boy held her at arm's length.

Poor Christian! Malise gone. His hero. His idol. Their chilly bedroom a contaminated temple.

He was, at least, at school during the day in term time and tending his vegetables at weekends and on summer evenings – but he was miserable, lonely and isolated. With floundering desire he tried to make friends with other pupils but nobody took much notice of him. One of the dingier masters, however, remarked that Christian had a melodious singing voice and invited him to join the church choir. It met only once a fortnight for practice in a wooden hall and he was driven there and back each time by his stepmother. She did nothing without a sigh and an indication that her duty was being done. Nearly every time she told Christian 'Your Daddy is very proud that you have joined the choir.'

At choir practice he again failed to get nearer to any of the boys or girls. He just sang louder and louder until he was ordered to lower his voice. One evening, however, a miracle occurred. The master who had invited him to join the choir also invited him to become a member of the local boy scouts.

Malise's absence during term time was an agony to him but the feeble crushes he formed, at school and at scouts, gave him hope even though, as happened each time, nobody responded to his overtures.

The church hall (known as the Mission Room) was dismal and cold. The piano, a tinkling, reedy instrument, rattled and seldom more than six singers (none of them as tuneful as Christian) came to practice. The choir master, the one whom had also invited him to join the scouts, had a speech impediment. Every time he uttered the hard letter 'c' it resounded like a pistol shot. Christ. Christmas. Christian. Choir. This impediment drew Christian instinctively towards the choirmaster.

Scouts took him to camp for a whole week. Each difficult word uttered by the master – club and camp – made the boys giggle. Poor Christian was uncertain as to which side to champion. Nobody wanted to bond.

Malises's holidays from school became the focus of his being. His dreams and desires lay in the prospect of rolling around with his brother on the linoleum in the dark.

When Malise returned from school for the holidays his need to use his brother as a sex object had disappeared. Evaporated. No further interest. The overhead light was turned off but nothing happened. Malise, clearing his throat, ordered Christian to put away his childish things. He, himself, had, he announced, become a man although Teddy bears were still permitted.

3

Malise enjoyed boarding school. Many of the boys and several of the masters fell for him; his looks, his composure, his lofty manner. He, too, joined a choir but his was a majestic one and boys sang to a world class organ. He revelled in ancient church music. It reminded him dimly of his mother, although he never thought of his father or Christian or of the upheavals he might have caused at home.

There were certain things that he found rather wonderful at school – particularly the boys bathing room where half a dozen tubs stood in two rows, all in sight of each other. No cordoning off. Older boys gazed in his direction. One of the masters, a Mr Scarlatti became besotted with him and allowed him the use of a spare shed in the school grounds. Malise had begun to show an interest in mechanical objects (not unlike himself) and told Mr Scarlatti that he needed a motor bicycle to tinker with in his spare hours. The master rescued one from a scrap heap and handed Malise enough cash with which to buy spare parts. His parts, too, he felt, were spare and he intended to continue being sparing with them as he resisted advances from boys and teachers. He became conceited – treating the motor cycle as he had treated Christian in their early childhood – riding it as an inanimate object. Mr Scarlatti would watch, glowing with pride, from a corner of the shed. 'You'll be a scientist my boy. One day we will see you in lights. Film star. Singer. Politician. Who knows? You are capable of big things.'

Malise paid him little attention. Nor did he pay much attention to learning. He seldom wrote to his father and never to his brother.

4

Christian began, in a limited fashion, to enjoy the company of his step-mother. He liked to help her make a shopping list that included coloured spills to help with lighting the fire – not that they lit it other than on Saturday evenings. On weekdays and on Sundays it was a four-barred electric heater that kept the sitting room warm. He helped Alyson to wash up dishes and to polish pieces of crested silver.

'Remember Christian' she often said as she wore a happy smile, 'Remember if things don't always seem to be bright, remember who you are. I, of course, wasn't born a Mc Hip but when I married your daddy I was honoured to become one. It might help to recall that you have roots in the aristocracy.'

'What are woots?' he asked, puzzled, as they walked the dog. Alyson began on a tedious explanation of his connections with a ducal family before he lost interest.

He often had problems in understanding what she said. She tended to sigh and complain about 'them.'

'What they say' – 'What they think' – 'What they want.' Christian tried hard to work out who 'they' might be – knowing few people as he did.

He preferred to walk alone through vast farm buildings where swallows swirled above him in summer months. He also much enjoyed watching a sty full of pigs as they stank and gobbled at vegetable stalks – and remembered, wistfully, how Malise had repeatedly told him, 'It's ridiculous how people talk of pigs as being dirty animals. The truth is quite the reverse. They are the very opposite.'

Christian had never understood those words – pigs looked filthy to him – but he knew his brother always to tell the truth.

There were two major treats each week. On Saturdays, at tea time in the sitting room, no wireless in the nursery, he listened with Alyson and his father to a weekly installment of Just William. It was terrifically exciting as the male announcer stopped before uttering the last word whereupon a female voice took over and called, desperately and highly pitched, the name 'William.' Her cry was long, drawn-out and added a kick to the programme. At such times, Christian was pleased that Malise was away – for his brother despised 'such dwivel.'

The other highlight was also a wireless programme called Monday Night at Eight O'clock. He listened to that alone with Alyson who told him each time. 'Daddy has gone off to the nursery with what they call his maps and with Malise's last letter.'

Being on a Monday, they didn't light the fire but, in winter, allowed themselves the use of the four-barred electric heater.

It was on the Home Service and, although the wireless crackled, the interviews, the musical break, the short detective play and the quizzes were entirely absorbing.

Christian believed himself to be part of the show and acted in rhythm to the tuneful start. He sang loud and well.

'It's Monday night at eight o'clock
Oh! Can't you hear the chimes?
Telling you to take an easy chair
Settle by the fireside, take out your *Radio Times*
For Monday Night at Eight is on the air.'

Alyson never tried to hush him but murmured 'they say it's educational.'

Thus the school terms went on. Christian joined Alyson on her shopping days at the local Co-operative store. There was a plaque there that read

All my neighbours, all my friends
Enjoy their Coop dividends
But I have been a foolish shopper
And haven't saved a single copper.'

'So Christian' his step mother assured him as she tucked her shopping into a vast leather bag, 'We are not foolish shoppers, as they say.'

5

Many weeks and months were struggled through, but
Christian's heart missed several beats as a certain summer
holiday drew near. He cancelled all choir practices and
camps. Eight weeks or thereabouts with Malise to hand.
Their romps had, of course, come to an end but the hero
worship endured.

He was destined to join him at boarding school when
these particular holidays were over.

Christian, Alyson and the dog (a black Labrador called
Digger) met Malise at the station all of eight miles away.
Malise had spent one night with a cousin of Alyson's in
Hampstead on his way back from school. He was tall even
though his growth spurt hadn't completed. His father and
Alyson had planned that he visit a London branch of an
Edinburgh tailor in order to be fitted for a kilt. By
Christmas it was likely that he would be invited to more
than one local 'hop.'

Now sixteen, Malise surveyed the farm house as the car

turned into the drive. Wysteria dripped over the porch. At foot level by the front door, stood a wrought-iron shoe-scraper and a giant cannonball. He awoke to the fact that it was not altogether an undesirable place. Farm buildings, cottages, antiquity. His father had already been old when he was born. It was certain, one day, to belong to him. He'd see to it that Christian and Alyson were both suitably housed in farm cottages. Standing to full height, he planned to pull his weight and to behave with correctitude. He was delighted by his looks and the prospect of a professionally put-together kilt (with sporran and socks) to be sent to the farm in good time for the Christmas holidays to start. Christian followed him around and occasionally, when he dared, asked what was likely to become of him when he joined his brother at boarding school the following term.

'Don't fwet Chwissy.' Malise smiled. 'We have to fend for ourselves in the big world. No more sitting around listening to Just William.'

Most days Malise wandered in the garden and took stock of its charm – noting that it was extremely well tended. It was filled with a mixture of flowers, vegetables, (mostly looked after by Christian), bamboos, grasses and fruit trees. He had learnt that it was almost entirely cared for by one toothless old man. Not extravagant, he noted. Alyson did her bit and even the ageing father pruned roses in summer months. The trees were fluffed out with blossom and the smell of lilies was stupefying. Against one wall stood a creaking greenhouse, bulging with ripening grapes. Altogether a reasonable inheritance. Nothing tremendous, of course, but some of his school mates lived in town terraces.

One afternoon he heard Alyson say, as she led a visiting neighbour, a Mrs Ruggles who came to take cuttings, round the paths 'We own, they say, two hundred acres.'

The Ruggles family owned two thousand acres and lived in a truly impressive house. Mrs Ruggles had smiled in discreet pride as Alyson told her about their modest plot and Malise squirmed with shame on behalf of his father and his illustrious ancestors.

Malise's mother's teaching had not taken root and, only last term, he had responded to a tract, smuggled in by Mr Scarlatti, on positive atheism by Bertrand Russell. This tract told him that his mother had barked up the wrong tree. Christian would do well to change his name. His own was less telling to the world at large.

6

Christian, clutching his Teddy bear, was terrified. He started his first term at boarding school while Malise made it clear that they were to see little of each other. 'Learn to stand on your own two feet', he advised as the train stopped at the school station before they shuffled off it with their trunks.

Mr Scarlatti, frustrated to a point of near madness by the emotional remoteness of his protégé, (although rewarded to have interested him in the works of Bertrand Russell and to have, therefore, something with him to discuss – in however a stately way) was dreadfully disappointed by the appearance of his brother. He was not entirely sure what he had expected. What he saw was a boy, low-browed, ruddy-cheeked, and lacking in coordination. Shy, awkward and unhappy. A poor replica of the Adonis he had come to worship.

Nothing much developed for any of them during that term. Mr Scarlatti's disappointment, Malise's interest in atheism and Christian's lonely misery were the features that distinguished it from other terms.

At home, Alyson made suggestions as her husband listened obediently.

'Don't you think, dear, it's time that Malise mixed with some of the young round here? He will, by the time the Christmas holidays come round, have that lovely kilt and I am willing, as you know, to drive him to any local hops.'

She had actually already heard about a 'hop' to take place during Christmas week. It was to be thrown by Mrs Ruggles (the one who Alyson had boasted to about her two hundred acres) and it was known that Mrs Ruggles was frantic to gather in some boys to partner her daughter and two of her nieces. Some suitable 'lads'.

The term moved slowly for both boys. For Christian because he was homesick. For Malise due to impatience after hearing from Alyson that he had been invited to no fewer than two 'hops' in the holidays, by which time his kilt would have arrived.

'They say' Alyson had written 'That the Ruggleses live in some style and it will be a good introduction for you in this part of the world.'

7

The evening of the 'hop' came round. As luck went, it was on a Monday evening and Alyson, having driven Malise to the Ruggles's house, was able to get back in time to listen, with Christian, to their favourite programme after making him a mug of Ovaltine.

Earlier, Alyson had learnt that reels were going to be danced and had passed the news on to her stepson by postcard. Malise had, with the help of Mr Scarlatti – who strained every muscle in his body in order to please – discovered a Scottish reel expert to teach steps in secret towards the end of the term. He learnt how to dance some of the more popular ones and became particularly expert at reversing.

With Alyson at the wheel, they followed a drive, flanked by iron railings, to a sweep in front of a house that had once been a small manor – added to before the first war to produce several handsome panelled rooms and some columns at the front.

Once inside, Malise was much taken by a large hall from which a staircase wound up. A great fire roared. There were several heads of game on the walls, bunches of holly hanging from them. A tall tree stood in the well of the stairs, an angel on the top. He was greeted by Mrs Ruggles – all curls and teeth – as Alyson slipped away.

The hostess, as were others, were astounded by Malise's appearance. More handsome than any had, or had ever expected, to see. He was contented in his kilt. All guests were offered fruit cup and vol-au-vents. 'To warm you up' Mrs Ruggles said although both the cup and the vol-au-vents were cold. Mr Ruggles was nowhere to be seen.

After the introductions (there were more girls than boys and one or two of the girls wore white frocks and coloured sashes – ready for reels) they were all summoned into a large room in which the carpet had been rolled back. There was a huge radiogram in there and by its side stood a lad, the gardener's son who manned it, dropping in eight records at one go.

The music began and Mrs Ruggles touched Malise's arm. 'The one with the blue sash. You can partner her for the Gay Gordons.' She was already a bit rattled and picked out the first girl who looked animated.

His kilt rippled as he kept impeccable time, paying particular attention to his reversing skills. The girl with the blue sash did well too and, when the reels were over, they sat together and sipped fruit cup and ate more of the vol-au-vents – ignoring all others.

The girl, not more than fifteen years old, wriggled and squirmed as they talked of local spots. Her lips parted and her bosom heaved as she lost her being in the aura of the handsomest boy she had ever seen – even in advertisements.

Reels were over and the gardener's son, much enjoying himself, plopped dance tunes, a Viennese Waltz or two included, into the machine. Shy and agonised teenagers moved again towards the patch of floor from which the carpet had been rolled up. Several girls were left without partners (the hostess's daughter and one of the visiting nieces among them) and talked frenziedly to each other as they stuffed more and more vol-au-vents between their discreetly painted lips.

Malise signalled to the girl by his side. 'Shall we tread a gay measure?'

He decided that he was not the sort of partner who cared to talk while dancing but wished to fit himself to a correct style with a flourish at the turns. They danced and Malise held the girl, whose name was Dawn, around her waist. She began to writhe, to heave and to quiver all over. Steamed and all but exploded as Malise realized that he was having trouble beneath his kilt. Noticing no others, the pair sweated and became ecstatic. They danced and danced – Dawn in a state of bewildered blindness;|Malise not bewildered exactly – but blind to surroundings. This went on until Mrs Ruggles announced 'Now. Dancing over.'

She had spotted the writhing but showed no outward sign of anguish other than to send a message via one of her daughters to Mr Ruggles who hid in his study. His presence was needed immediately.

A sheepish and diminutive Mr Ruggles, at the side of his wife, spoke hesitantly. 'Dancing over and now a bit more to eat before your parents join us all for a nightcap and then take you all home.'

Malise gave Dawn a vague look – as to bestow a promise. He forced his eyes to water as they gazed into hers.

'Here come the parent-birds' Mrs Ruggles shouted as the front door opened and middle aged couples – Alyson among them – arrived, bringing with them an icy draught.

Alyson had no idea why Mrs Ruggles was less friendly than before but did not query Malise's social skills.

After fruit salad and meringues, the fathers were offered a glass of whisky each by the unwilling and desiccated Mr Ruggles.

Alyson, her double chin wobbling, wanted to hear more about the evening as they sat beside each other in the car but Malise was still uncomfortable in his kilt and offered little in the way of answer.

'Did you join in the reels dear?'

'Yes. Yes. I did.'

'One or two of the girls were pretty weren't they?'

'Yes. Yes. They were.'

'I expect you enjoyed the music and getting to know some neighbours.'

'Yes. Yes. I did.'

Small reward for all the ferrying she had done.

After he had folded his clothes in the bathroom, Malise placed the sporran beside the kilt and noticed a scrap of paper peeping from it. It gave the name 'Dawn Willis' as well as an address. She did, he realised, live not unreasonably far away.

When he had cleaned his teeth he called out to Alyson who was in the passage wearing a pink bath cap, 'Did you say there was to be another 'hop' before Christmas?'

'Yes dear. I'm pleased you enjoyed it. The next one won't be quite as splendid as the Ruggleses but it will do you good to mingle with the young again. It's a lovely neighbourhood.'

Christian pretended to be asleep when Malise switched on the overhead light. Although Alyson had always done her best to mother the boys she had never got round to helping them out with bedside lamps. Malise had removed his copy of the Bible – once hopefully placed beside his bed by his mother. It had been replaced by Bertrand Russell's *Why I Am Not A Christian*.

Christian's much studied holy book still sat on his spindly table. As did his Teddy bear.

8

Christmas drew near. Alyson answered the telephone as the four of them lunched in the kitchen. The others heard her say 'No sign of it here. Well. You may be right. Better safe than sorry but Malise will be disappointed.'

The second 'hop' had been cancelled owing to the threat of a snow storm. Nothing had been forecast on the wireless. Malise was perplexed, as were they all.

Alyson tried to comfort him. 'They say it might be here in time for Christmas. I daresay they didn't want to risk it.'

He decided to call on Dawn. He had looked up her address on an ordnance survey map – translating it from the poorly written scrap she had popped into his sporran.

Wearing boots but with shoes strung around his neck, he set forth. He pulled on his only overcoat – dark brown and with a belt across the back of it. Might Dawn come to life again as she had on the dance floor? Having walked for two miles he arrived at the front door of a farm house – a large one – not unlike the one he proposed to own.

Perhaps the farms matched? He rang the bell. Dawn's father came to the door and instantly recognised Malise. He had been the parent to fetch his daughter from the Ruggles's 'hop' and realised that there stood the young man to have so disturbed Dawn that fatal evening. She had not been the same since. Her simpering, pert prettiness had faded into a grumpy, pasty one and she seldom spoke.

'Hello there,' he said.

Malise, thrown by the look he was given, cleared his throat and asked if he might be granted a moment with the daughter of the house.

Dawn's father made as if to shut the door on him but Malise hadn't finished.

'Might you know if your daughter is to attend the party tomorrow? People called Haslip?'

Door still open by a crack, he answered 'yes, as far as I know. Is that all?'

It wasn't snowing and it didn't look as if it was going to.

He trudged, deflated almost for the first time in his life, across the fields.

As he swung himself over a style he heard Dawn panting up behind him and squeaking slightly. She caught up and, after they had both crossed the style, he hooked her arm in his – as curious to see her in woolly clothing as she was to see him without his kilt. It neared the shortest day of the year.

His home barn was as likely to be as safe as anywhere unless, by unlucky chance, Christian lurked around there.

Malise tried a joke. 'What about a bit of a barn dance?'

Dawn needed no joke to encourage her.

The inside of the barn was cold, dark and

uncomfortable. A scary bull looked in from the paddock but there was no sign of Christian lurking.

Malise left his shoes there for later collection. No point in carrying them to and fro. He walked Dawn home, or nearly. Not near enough to be spotted by her father. He promised to write to her but never did so.

9

'Malise. We were looking for you dear.' Alyson was agitated. 'It's after six and dark.'

The cancellation of the second 'hop' remained a puzzle at the farmhouse and it was not until many months later that she discovered it to have taken place. By that time it was too late to make attempts to get to the bottom of the mystery.

Nothing startling happened to either boy during the following two terms or holidays. Malise was a trifle nervous of being tracked down by Dawn when he was at home. He hankered after her body but dreaded her company. He was safe, however, for she had been placed under strict curfew by her parents when it was known that the young 'neighbours' were around.

Malise was grateful to Dawn for proving to him that he would, at a later stage, be able to interact with girls and imagined himself cutting a dash at debutante parties when the moment came in the not too distant future. With his looks and lineage he was sure to get many invitations.

But, by the summer of 1937, there were threats of war. A terrible war seemed likely.

To Mr Scarlatti's sorrow, Malise had not done well in his studies. Besides the motorbike, he had developed an almost obsessive interest in atheism combined with science. His examination results were poor. That, however, made little difference to the lottery of his future for, before the end of his school-leaving year, he had been called up and sent to a military training camp where he clean forgot to ponder on the views and fate of Bertrand Russell.

10

Malise was interviewed for a rifle regiment and started, democratically, at a barracks near Lewes in Sussex. Until that time he had never felt affection for anyone. His family were passable and Mr Scarlatti had been useful but not one amongst them had ever excited his sympathy.

He appeared haughty. At his first inspection the Sergeant Major asked 'has a camel been shitting on your boots?'

Malise was taken aback by that. His boots were perfectly clean and he imagined the man to be joking so, clearing his throat as was his wont, he decided to reply in the same vein.

'Yes Sergeant. I bumped into one outside the latrine.' That went down badly. The Sergeant Major sneered at him and told him not to be facetious. Malise almost accepted, then, that he was no good at jokes.

His emotions had been underfed and stunted by his bible-bashing mother, his silent and withdrawn father, his heavily built step-mother and his slow, simple doting

brother. Not that Christian was exactly stupid. He had
begun to show signs of ability to learn in some areas and
occasional flickers of sly cunning shone in his dull eyes.

Later at a training Battalion in the North, Malise found
himself swallowed up in mechanical tasks that interested
him and in daily contact with boys from a very different
background to the one he had known.

It was uncomfortable and there were many rough cadets
– but he got on well enough with them. He began to be
accepted although his looks and demeanour were
intimidating. One night a boy urinated all over his face
whilst the others gathered round the hard bed and asked,
'What do you think of us lot?'

Malise, not knowing where he had picked up such
language, answered 'I think you are all bloody, fucking
idiots,' whereupon they all clapped and said 'He's one of us
after all.' That was the nearest moment that Malise had ever
come to happiness.

Then came the war. He was called up.

He lived through horrible things. Death, wounds, guns,
tanks, pain and despair. For much of that time he was in
Italy as retreating Germans fought back. His kilt and Dawn
were almost forgotten but not the memory of experiences
on the dance floor or in his father's barn. He often pined
for a woman's body and, by chance, occasionally found one
on farms in Italy. He took a great fancy to Italy and to the
courage and virtues of its inhabitants – although he
deplored the fact that so many cigarettes were smoked by
the denizens of that, otherwise, magical country.

11

He returned, a young and handsome man, as a Captain and with the brotherhood of war swiftly forgotten.

Back at the farm it was clear that he was expected to sleep in his old, shared bedroom.

Christian, although he had worked sturdily and single-handedly on the farm, had become stout. His eyes were not strong and he had been excused from the army – sleeping alone in his double bedroom but for the Bible and the Teddy bear. He had though, when summoned, done his bit for the Home Guard and a letter of thanks from a local authority, framed by himself, was propped up on the table between the beds.

It read 'Dear Mr Mc Hip, Now that hostilities are over we want to send you a little token present in gratitude and pride for all you have been doing in these long years of war and we ask you to accept the enclosed postal order for thirty shillings with our best wishes for a time of prosperity and peace.'

Malise sneered and asked, 'what did you do when I was fighting? Cleaned out the odd ditch and walked the dog, I suppose.'

'Walked the dog? I wondered when you were going to notice that Digger is no more.'

'Apologies. What became of him?'

'Choked on a bit of cheese we think. Alyson let a chunk drop and Digger wolfed it down. Nothing we could do to save him. Poor old hound. Alyson was cut up but wouldn't hear of getting another one.'

Malise sympathized with Alyson when next they met.

'Commiserations on the loss of Digger. 'I'd be happy, ahem, to acquire a replacement.'

'Thank you dear – but no thank you. Not at our age. Not fair on an animal they say.'

Christian's slight artfulness, as first displayed some years after becoming a school boarder, had grown stronger – had almost developed into cunning. This was accompanied by lack of fear for his brother. He left the trophy exactly where it had been placed and offered no reply to Malise's taunt.

Alyson had a stiff hip, (it comforted her a little to remember that, by marriage, she was a Mc Hip) and her husband was more bowed and withdrawn than before.

The house had become dusty and rank during years of war shortages. A cupboard under the stairs was stuffed with dark, floppy gas masks. Around the place were odd, spiky lumps of shrapnel (called 'shwapnel' by Christian who had picked them up in the farm yard). Although the farm was rural, it was not far from London and doodlebugs had flown overhead. Fields nearby were topsy turvy with bomb crates and many of the windows showed traces of brownish, sticky paper – plastered over panes to prevent glass from shattering. Ills of war showed all around.

Alyson got Christian to open a bottle of wine to celebrate Malise's return.

'To the gallant Captain', she said 'We are proud of you and, they say, it's brave lads like you who have fought to free us all.'

It was summer and the garden had been neglected. Not that Christian hadn't struggled with the vegetable plot. The old gardener had died and the place was unkempt.

Malise had no plan. He did not want to stay at home, sharing a room with his less than besotted brother. He formed the idea of going to London when things were settled. An income had filtered through to him from a family trust. It would provide enough, if frugal (which he certainly was) for him to manage without earning.

Many of his leisure hours were spent in writing to old school contemporaries; some from the army too. He wrote neatly in italics and hoped to hook up in a shared flat somewhere central if possible.

There was enough money for him to buy good shoes, a dinner jacket, a smart suit and a second hand car.

As the family gloated over his safe return, he planned his escape.

One morning Alyson said 'I'm going to drive along to Samstead. There's a bit of petrol in the Harvest Gold. It will be lovely to see a wedding. None of us have been asked which is disappointing as it's local. Too many relatives, I expect. They say that everyone has chipped in with clothing coupons to help with the bride's frock.'

'Whose wedding is it?' Malise asked. Normally he took no interest in Alyson's words.

'The Willis girl. Dawn, I believe her name is. Marrying a lad from Essex. Not far off.'

'I'll drive you' he said. Alyson was amazed. Amazed and thrilled. Perhaps he viewed her as a second mother after all. Perhaps the war had softened him towards her.

They drove slowly and not at all far. Church bells rang and the sun brightened as Dawn and her father stepped from the bridal car to walk the path towards an old flint church. Malise, alongside Alyson, watched from the lane – Malise suffocating an inner wince at the memory of his last and only encounter with the, now top-hatted Mr Willis. They did not see much of the bride as she was surrounded by bridesmaids and fussing females.

'Shall we go home dear? The service is sure to last an hour at least.'

Malise, who wore a bright blue open shirt, chosen to match his eyes, wanted to stay and see the group leave the church after the ceremony. He wished to witness Dawn's triumphant exit as a married woman – groom at her side. He might just catch her eye. Disturb her in some small way before she set off on her honeymoon.

He suggested taking a walk. It was a fine day and, although Alyson had trouble with her hip and needed the support of a stick, she was pleased that the handsome Captain wished to spend an hour walking with her – so she put up no argument.

They walked, extremely slowly, through the village, past thatched cottages, their gardens alive with honeysuckle and roses.

They were once again outside the church where a sprinkling of people gathered to rejoice with the happy couple. Bells rang again. Pauses for photographs. Clusters of bridesmaids in the porch.

Down the path came Dawn in bridal white on the arm of her husband. Malise stepped near to the spot that they planned to pass. He drew his handsome head high out of and above the blue shirt and stared her in both eyes. He noticed her startle as she smiled to the waiting watchers. He turned to Alyson, much pleased with Dawn's unprepared look. Keep the bridegroom on his toes.

'Pretty bride' he said.

'Yes. They say she was a little on the fast side. I daresay her people are pleased she has found a nice young man.'

12

Life was dingy at home. Malise became increasingly irritated by the way the farmhouse was run. Packets of pills stood unashamedly propped by the clock on the mantel piece. Nescafé, newly popular, alongside crumpled brown paper bags, lay on the chest in the hall. Little method. Skimpily sliced ham, tinned spam and, most often, a baked potato with a dab of margarine topping it, for lunch. Toasted cheese (Alyson called it Welsh Rarebit) for supper. Seldom wine. Sometimes cider. Food was rationed and bought at the Co-operative Store.

Malise, with occasional trips to London on bleak trains to Liverpool Street Station, did as little as possible to help but advised on detail as Christian worked, a little half-heartedly, on the farm and in the garden.

The loss of Christian's admiration and praise puzzled and disturbed Malise. The younger man had taken to answering back. Not only answering back but to asking peculiar questions.

'So Malise. Do you see yourself taking a wife?'

'A wife. Whose?' Malise still enjoyed a stately joke.

'Your own I mean. After all. You are the wight age. I need to know because, if you never have childwen, I daresay the farm will go to me. That's if you die first of course.'

Malise was dumbfounded by Christian's attitude and began to wonder whether to look for a suitable bride in London. All the same, whatever Christian's new views, the idea of sharing his life was unimaginable.

Advice had been given on clothes by a distant cousin to whom Malise had written and who worked at the House of Lords. In reply to his letter the cousin had suggested Lobb's in St James's Street for shoes. That or Ticker in Jermyn Street. He had also recommended a tailor called Lesley & Roberts in Savile Row.

On day trips to London Malise visited the shoemaker and had a 'last' made of his feet – a sort of model in wood. He was pleased by the skill that went into it but appalled by the expense. Nonetheless he ordered two pairs of shoes – one black and one brown. Suits (one dark, one tweed) were fitted. Also a dinner jacket. He was jubilant.

Most of the letters had remained unanswered but one showed promise. It came from a man who had been a year or two younger than Malise at school and who he remembered as being one of the many who had hero-worshipped him. He was called Alex James and now had a job in the city and rented a flat in Pimlico. At the moment he shared with another school friend and they were looking for a third.

13

Much time was taken up with preparation. Malise poured, meticulously, over money matters and found that it was possible (out of income) to pay for the new clothes and his share of rent and food in the Pimlico flat. He would have to look for some form of employment – even if unpaid.

During these long days, the loss of Christian's besottedness was his chief bugbear. He had never deciphered a warning but had believed the brotherly love to be indissoluble; unshakeable. Both men were shut to reason. His thoughts sometimes told him that Christian held a hammer over his head; threatened him in a loutish way. He knew Christian to have always been a misfit, lonely, doing heaven knew what with boy scouts, but, whatever else, eternally rapturous as disciple.

Now Christian was supposing himself to be responsible for the possible future of the family line – however remote from the centre of ducal power. Leader of the McHips. Hip Hip Hooray. It was outrageous. Malise had always outshone and destabilised his brother into weakness.

After more dreary months at the farm he was all set for Pimlico. Not long before his departure he had seen, with Christian who had needed persuasion when it came to accompanying him, an Ealing Studio comedy. *Passport to Pimlico*. Christian had pronounced it 'tewwibly funny.' Malise had enjoyed it too – even if uneasy in Christian's reluctant company – and considered his viewing of it fortuitous, what with his decision to move to the area.

After agonising negotiations, he bought himself a dark green, second hand Lagonda and tinkered with it as lovingly as he had done with his motorbike at school. He christened it 'Ruggles' – a tribute to the family responsible for the 'hop' where Dawn had responded with such liveliness to his kilt. Hop. Hip. Mc Hip.

Before departure he packed all his expensive clothing. He also heaped a rustic basket full with withered apples from Alyson's stored rack.

14

He arrived at the Pimlico ground floor flat, unloaded his car and thrust the apples at one of his future sharers and asked for the basket to be returned. Alex was surprised. He had in store several tins of peaches in syrup and they seemed to be adequate for supper parties. He did not appear to remember having had a crush on Malise at school and Malise certainly would not have remembered him had they met elsewhere.

He looked at his room and approved. Uninteresting, but possibly answering his needs. Almost to his liking. A small room with a small bed. Small bed. Hmm.

As it happened he stayed in that small room for several years.

He managed to persuade his cousin at the House of Lords to allow him to run, although without payment, a few errands. Thus he was able to say, looking mysterious, that he had something to do with the Upper House.

After that first journey he drove the car back and left it

at the farm.

Every month or so he returned home – always by train. It meant travelling by underground to Liverpool Street Station . He disliked the journey because almost everyone smoked and it was cloudy and stank. Tobacco had, although unacceptable anywhere, struck him as less seedy when smoked in Italy.

He did, however, enjoy some of the advertisements. One in particular. There was a wispy picture of a girl in bridal dress looking happy and prepared for her wedding day. Under it was written '… and Berlei sheets will do the rest.' He knew, full well, that unless he found an heiress with quarterings, he was not destined to 'do the rest.' The realisation, since Christian's defection, made him a trifle uneasy.

Christian always met him at the station and asked, but showing no enthusiasm, 'So. How is the big, bad city?'

Christian's life had improved. He was free of thraldom to Malise , the choir was reformed and senior scouts provided him with unsteady excitements.

Malise, irked, decided to try returning to his old masterly ways. Shock tactics. Possibly turn the clock back.

'So Cwissy. Now you seem to think you are worthy to gather up the cwumbs.'

'Cwumbs. That's about it. I'll give you cwumbs.'

No headway.

Alyson was lamer. The father more bent.

Apart from sporadic unease when brooding over Christian, these were happy times for Malise. He saw little of his London flat mates and found them easy to share with. Occasionally he ate in with one or other of them.

Each had a regular girlfriend and sometimes brought one home for supper. Meals always ended with tinned peaches – sometimes brandy added and sometimes a tube of condensed milk. Malise liked coming in to find one or other of the courting couples on the small sofa in the sitting room. It amused him to see if he could disturb the girl into some sort of interest in him before, politely, retiring to his room to read about the Etruscans in whose history he had become doggedly intrigued. He never managed breaking a romance up, though. He felt it was because he did not try hard enough. He disliked sharing a bathroom in which he did a lot of gargling and screwed tops onto tooth-paste tubes (this reminded him of his mother and then, uneasily, of Christian when pinned to the floor) left on the basin by the others – before walking to the House of Lords in search of errands. Sometimes there were none but one of the secretaries was pretty. Solitude was necessary to him and he walked a great deal in London, scheming as he went.

There was a network afoot in the social world and Malise managed to get himself on to some vital lists. Debutante balls were revitalised and, with his looks and his being associated, however spuriously, with The House of Lords, hostesses showed an interest in him. A redoubtable lady called Jennifer worked for the *Tatler* magazine and helped debutantes' mothers when compiling lists for coming-out dances.

There were no black marks against his name, even though his advancing age might have told against him. Some of the boys had NSIT next to their names – warning girls that they were not safe in taxis should they offer a lift home after a dance. Malise had never been in a taxi, nor did he plan to break the habit, safe in it or not. A small part of him disapproved of the loss of war time equality – as smart London revived to distance itself from the memory of servantless days – but he knew where he rightfully belonged.

Before each dance there was always a dinner party – held in the house or flat of a debutante's mother and/or father – depending on their situations in marriage.

There were usually about ten guests, gender matched, at these dinners and many of the young men were recruited by Jennifer from an army camp at Windsor. Malise was older than the average young man. Conversation could be sticky. Young men were expected to ask the young ladies they had been seated next to at dinner to dance when they arrived at the ball.

Often these balls took place at hotels. The Savoy River Room, The Hyde Park Hotel, Claridge's. Malise was always wary for fear of being expected to escort a girl home. Not that he didn't often fancy one. He liked to walk back to Pimlico – often in breezy contentment after having made a conquest.

More often than not, they danced to the music of Tommy Kinsman's band. Kinsman was a lively, short, spirited bandleader. Some of the plainer girls got to know him well and often, noisily, plucked, when needed, a partner from his troupe.

One evening, at The Hyde Park Hotel, Malise danced with a beautiful girl. She did not match up to Dawn's lack of restraint on the floor but, after they had danced close to the strains of ' Mountain Greenery' she was not to be the same for years to come. Her knees were weak and her eyes enormous. Malise clasped her round the waist and pressed his cheek to hers. He had to bend a bit as he was tall. She did not quite have an orgasm as had Dawn – and he did not wear a kilt. Nonetheless she was unsettled.

When the beauty drifted away to powder her nose – her eyes showing him that, before minutes were up, she would be back in his arms for the next dance, he nipped down the stairs and was away. The band struck up with 'Some Enchanted Evening' as the girl made frantic searches for her partner. He had been doing no more than keeping his hand, or whatever, in.

Although he lacked ease of manner, Malise was invited to many of these parties. He tended to give courtly bows and to force jokes. These traits held him up with the more sophisticated girls. Some even pronounced him 'creepy.' He was unable to talk naturally. His words were composed, resulting in a failed air of spontaneity.

On free evenings, he sometimes went to the cinema. He never met with a friend or relation; never invited a young lady to dine with him although he occasionally gave thought to the one who had swooned in his arms at The Hyde Park Hotel.

In spite of being conceited in some areas, he was aware of being a misfit, pedantic, stiff and lacking in feeling. He feared being seen as a cardboard character for his attempts at mixing were awkward. He did have a scholarly side and wished that he hadn't been in love with a motorcycle when at school.

When not doing his slight job, he spent many hours at the British Museum reading about Etruscans and, in other spare time, redeveloping his anti-clericalism.

He stuck to his budget and convinced himself that he was not at his imaginary best without eight hours of sleep each night.

15

He was well over thirty by the time he knew that he had to make a change. Visits to the farm, with Christian silent and semi-hostile, became less and less appealing; visits to the British Museum Etruscan department, more and more so.

There he poured over funerary practices, language, customs and engravings of rock-cut chamber tombs.

He tired of, and knew that he was bad at, social life. Hostesses tumbled to the fact that he was never likely to marry their daughters. He did hear, twice by letter, from his 'conquest' at The Hyde Park Hotel but did not reply. She must have winkled out his address with the help of Jennifer who still worked for the *Tatler* magazine.

With a friendly, youngish Italian man, Giovanni, who worked at the museum, he heard of a small flat that he might be able to rent in Volterra. The Italian man's aunt was no longer able to live alone there and the flat was about to become empty. Malise thought he would be able to survive on his income and yearned to buy fresh comestibles (as he called food) from local markets.

That part of Italy had been dreadfully short of provisions during the war but, or so he had heard, quantity and quality had flooded back.

His mind was filled with cheeses, figs, salami, grapes and peaches. Not tinned ones in syrup. He pictured himself walking to the Etruscan Museum – might even land a small job there. Money posed a possible problem but ways could be found. Exchange was tricky. Basil, bars and Bolognese sauce. Cappuccinos and carafes. He planned to drive Ruggles there. Petrol? Proscuitto, Parmesan and Prosecco. Not that he drank much in the way of alcohol. Moderation. Sticking his neck above his collar, he strained in front of the looking glass – rehearsing absurd words aloud.

Italy, he fully decided, in spite of the chain smoking, was the place for him. He had seen dead and dying there as Germans struggled to hold on, but he had not been unhappy. No social skills had been needed. It refreshed him to remember how little his lack of them had mattered. Not that he had then understood that he lacked them – or had even known about them.

His failure to produce favourable reactions puzzled and almost hurt him.

16

There were hiccoughs during discussions with his Italian friend at the museum. The aunt, believed likely to spend the rest of her days in a home for the sickly, had recovered her strength and a tenant was no longer needed for her apartment in Volterra.

It dealt a blow to Malise who was rearing to go but did not wish to pay *pensione* fees as he looked for a more permanent perch. Giovanni begged for patience when Malise showed dismay.

'I know the best place for you. Not Volterra but my cousin has a nice apartment for renting just now. In Lucca. A beautiful city. Little food in wartime but now in prosperity. It is not a long way – only two hours from Volterra so, if you take it, you can search from there.'

Giovanni lit a cigarette and talked in a low voice.

'Lucca, for me, is a fantastic place. There are many large and beautiful gardens within the walls. That is why the city survived well during war.'

His cigarette burnt low as he continued talking. 'For me, too, Lucca is special. My uncle was chief of police there. The Nazis ordered him to round up all Jews. I was only a boy. My uncle rounded them up – one day early – helping them on to trains and allowing them to escape. I don't know where they went. The next day the Nazis shot my uncle dead and my aunt took many pills to join him. In my family we are proud of this aunt and uncle.'

Giovanni looked sad and Malise remembered how near he had been to atrocity at the time. Not that the memory of his proximity to horror triggered off much in the way of sympathy or involvement.

The rent was low. The apartment was up seventy-nine steep steps – above a small piazza in the centre of the city; a city surrounded by walls – Part Medieval, part Roman.

'My cousin is living in Birmingham and the place is empty. You find it enchanting. That I am sure.'

Giovanni was hopeful and so, after a bit of thought, was Malise.

He decided to go ahead and, after some planning, set off in Ruggles.

With a proud, resolute certitude, he made a stately and rewarding entry into the city, under one of the gates that arched through the walls. There were few cars and Ruggles caused a satisfactory stir as he drove cautiously into the town. Many times he stopped and asked, in faltering Italian, for help with directions. Always he caused interest. He was able to park Ruggles in the *piazza* outside the entrance to the building near to the top of which his future apartment perched. Cats writhed round doorways. He looked up and noticed that his rooms were the highest. A basket hung from one of the top windows on a rope. Elevator for shopping. Picturesque, he decided. Bells, pigeons, walls, a Roman amphitheatre, cobbles, bakeries, flowers, an orthopaedic shop, a pet shop where a parrot spoke in Italian. Olive oil, honey, bicycles (few riders paying attention to the use of handle bars.)

The city, although short of food, had not been harmed during the war. Malise blanked the war out. He had the knack.

He learnt that Lucca had belonged to Napoleon and that he had given it to his sister. Had he had a sister, he would not have given it to her. Nor to a brother.

There was a forecourt below the apartment building where nobody stopped him leaving his car. It constantly amused him that he had named it 'Ruggles.' Again he thought back to his long past dance with Dawn in Mrs Ruggles's drawing room where the carpet had been rolled back. He, in his kilt, had all but been rolled back too and he revelled in that moment of the past. Even wondered how Dawn's marriage was going.

He saw himself as picturesque as he filled the basket with lentils, pastas and focaccia loaves before racing up the seventy nine steps, three at a time.

From the window, with immense satisfaction, he wound the rope upwards.

17

The apartment was charming, uncluttered, and looking out over red tiled roofs with mountains beyond. The building, all of old brick, was a simple duecento tenement one. Malise liked situating a year in its actual numbers. 'Duecento' seemed to him more immediate to the time than thirteenth century. He sat and read his guide book, from time to time looking out of the window.

The first night he was kept awake by the Torre delle Ore, a medieval bell that rang every quarter of an hour, confounding him by the oddness of the rings – for when, by his grandfather's Half Hunter watch, he saw midnight, the bells only rang six times. The strangeness of this was explained to him in the morning when, at a *pasticceria* he tried to make himself known as a regular by speaking Italian in arbitrary genders. He asked why bells that were meant to tell the time were so odd. The explanation, also quite odd, was that in the Middle Ages, bells rang only up to six, so, six in the morning, six at noon, six at six in the evening and six at midnight. He was learning fast.

It came to him. Bricks. A study of brickwork in Lucca was to become his interest. Esoteric. Unfashionable. Rarefied.

He set out each morning with a pencil and pad, to take notes and make drawings of bricks that formed arches and the lintels above doors and windows. His close studies led him to suppose that the earlier bricks – say of the thirteenth century – were decorated with simple rosettes and zigzags, but whose decorations became more and more complicated in the later bricks of the fifteenth century. The historian in him thought the earlier in time the better for the sincerity of simplicity whereas the later ones showed the decadence of complexity. After all the early ones were carved by hand and for the later ones a mould was used.

Thanks to a connection through some cousins, he did have a letter of introduction to la Contessa Isolata and, after having left it on her, received an invitation to her palazzo. She waited behind the servant, who opened the door, and held out her hand to him but dropped it as he reached for it and said 'piacere' which he had thought the proper expression on greeting (having been busy with a short-cut phrase book) but which, clearly, was not. She showed him into her *soggiorno* and asked him why he had come to live in Lucca. He replied, with a worldliness that was surely authentic enough to know what the proper expression was on greeting, that he was fascinated by brick. That was an important reason for his choosing to live in a duecento slum tenement.

'Brick?' she asked. He said 'It may be a presumption of mine to know more about your bricks than a Lucchese whose family have lived here for centuries but, you see, bricks are of great historical interest.'

'Are they?'

He offered to take her on a tour of Lucca to study the various brick work, from Roman through to Renaissance and even to the *Belle Époque*, but she declined as he made to leave. At the door, she held out her hand to shake his and said 'My dear Mr Mc Hip. I must warn you that it is difficult to get into *Lucchese* society although you do have the aristocratic credentials, but, if you do have such aspirations, never say *'piacere'* when introduced.

Malise stood, as if at attention, but did not ask why. The Contessa went on 'but how could you know, used, as you are, to your own manners? Here we do not say *'piacere.'*

'What, then, should I say?'

'Do as your compatriots do' the Contessa Isolata answered 'say nothing.'

He accepted that he was not in tune with social spheres *'piacere'* or not. It was bewildering and he did not see the Contessa again.

Apart from regretting his innocent solecism, the days passed gratifyingly and fast. He hired a bicycle and rode, stiff backed, through broad avenues around the ramparts.

He walked in the city, taking notes of its sensational sights. The vast wooden figure of Christ in the cathedral – borne by crewless ships from the Holy Land, it was said, and carried by driverless carts to Lucca. He believed not a word of the myth. He and Bertrand Russell thought otherwise and his mother had become no more than a pale and pious shadow.

He lived among the *Lucchese*; those who kept fruit and

vegetable stalls in the market, dug up old cobbles in the high street, the Via Fillungo (the long thread), to replace old sewage pipes or, on a higher level, sold religious articles in a shop near the Duomo.

His mistrust of religion in no way diminished his pleasure or prevented him from gazing at the shrivelled remains of Santa Zita, patron saint of serving maids, in the wondrous Romanesque church of San Frediano. She was barely more than bones but held plastic flowers and was decorated in colourful lace.

He liked to stride around a piazza built on the foundations of an old Roman amphitheatre where a Roman bath stood, filled with rotting tomatoes and where body-shaped washing hung from upper windows. Then to walk homewards over paved or cobbled streets, passing handsome, carved, wooden shop fronts.

Most of all he revelled in sitting in a corner of the grand piazza watching girls, many very pretty, as they chatted loudly to each other from the seats of their bicycles; most of them smoking cigarettes and few using handlebars.

It was not a large town and, after some months, many of the local people became familiar to him.

One in particular. She did not smoke.

On a certain day, that particular girl fell from her bicycle near to where Malise sat at a table of an outdoor bar.

He leapt from his chair. Good looks to the fore. 'Scusi *signorina*. Voglia Scusarmi.' He had again been busy with a phrase book and spoke in clipped Italian as he offered to pick her and her shopping up.

The girl, dark and slight, said 'I'm OK but thanks all the same.'

'You are English then?'

'I am. So are you.' She had recognised his accent.

'Yes.'

They laughed and he offered to buy her a cup of coffee. That or a Campari and soda. She parked her bicycle and sat with him, out of doors, in the magnificent piazza where pigeons strutted as they pecked at grain thrown to them by meticulously dressed, white socked, children.

She settled for a Campari and soda and they talked about their reasons for being there. He told her, with minor embellishments, murmuring about Etruscans and bricks. She was, she told him as she gazed at his handsome face, married to an Italian academic who worked at the university in Pisa. Pisa had been horrifyingly bombed in the war and Lucca was a more tranquil place in which to live. Much re-building going on in Pisa.

Malise found her entrancing. Brown eyes, faultless legs, curly mouth. She was quick and disconcertingly alert.

She, Patricia, found him to be unusual, educated and English. She was a trifle starved of Englishness. The handsomeness of his face was almost an introduction.

They got on well. She thanked him, picked up her parcels, retrieved her bicycle and rode away on it.

He then realised that, in his own eyes, he was not, after all, a mummified pedant. He even got a kick out of paying for the Campari and soda.

His heart had turned over. He went back, up his seventy-nine stairs and writhed about on the thin bed reliving the dance with Dawn (replacing her body with that of Patricia) when he had been sixteen. He always returned to that regardless of what might have taken place in intervening years.

18

His normally robust emotional system was disturbed. Mind, mixed and mingled, he disturbed himself and his bedding. He didn't dream because he didn't sleep but believed his hands to be investigating every beautiful curve of the girl who had fallen from her bicycle.

No thought for the academic husband. Up until that day he had considered himself to have become desiccated and odd.

Now he lived in the land of predators.

Waking was exciting but, uncharacteristically fearful of rejection were he and Patricia to meet, he made up his mind to drive to Volterra.

He had not attempted this outing during his time in Lucca – due to the lapsing of his interest in Etruscan history.

He drove through flat land before climbing into hills, cypress trees, tumbling buildings. Sheep, Stars of Bethlehem, white and sparkling on the roadside, as he rounded steep bends. Precipices sliding away from steep cliff. His brain and visual senses still seemed to be calmly at work even if other parts of him twitched. Great gates. The city was magnificent. Owls sheltered under umbrellas blinking at the hilly foundations that crumbled – having taken with them over the centuries, entire villages.

The museum, jammed with sarcophagi and elongated kitchen utensils from a forgotten civilisation, slightly bored him – although they were the cause of his being there in the first place.

He decided to write a guide book. Always room for a new one – brick work included – and it would give an accountable reason for his being there at all. He sat in the piazza and flipped through packets of torn and blotchy Italian bank notes. One hundred thousand by the one hundred thousand. He considered thwarting his desires and adding, with luck, to Patricia's curiosity by spending a night or two in that glorious hill-top town. There was a chance that she might bicycle through Lucca whilst keeping an eye out for him.

She might, even, one day, climb with him up the seventy-nine steps.

If, say, he stayed away for a few nights, (he counted the notes again) there was a possibility of her curiosity rising. Two nights in Volterra. The least expensive room to be found. But only an hour and a half in his car and he could be back in Lucca. Back at the bar. Back, maybe, in the presence of Patricia. He bought a newspaper. Anything to pass the time for Etruscan remains weren't holding his attention. Bicycles passed. Ladies' legs. He also went to the unusual length of buying a postcard to send to his father and Alyson. He excluded Christian. Teach him a lesson for his faithlessness.

He wrote 'Greetings from the world of Etruscan treasures!!' He was much addicted to screech marks. 'I'm keeping body and soul together as my limited budget requires, but am much absorbed in the intriguing past.'

He walked into the cathedral and was taken aback by the gaudily painted Deposizione – the startling figure of Christ as he was removed from the cross by giant tweezers. His was to be a quaint and quirky guide book.

But he drove back to Lucca. The pull was overpowering. There was a traffic hold up on the way – in the distressed and drab town of Pontedera – which delayed him for an hour or more – so he didn't get back to the city until late.

Streets were empty and bicycles no longer on them. He loved his own humanity as he trudged up the steps and ached for the next day to come.

He was becoming a spender and ate breakfast outside at the bar as he looked to the church with its ancient brick façade (between glances at the passing cyclists). She might be an early bird. Might shop before the heat descended.

Travesties of her cycled by – large ladies with red lips and navy blue hair. Squeaky voices. Cigarettes.

19

He quaked at the thought of deserting his post. Many times, as he tried to sit still, he semi-jumped. It was almost her – but never *her* enough. Pretty girls, plain girls – boys too – rode past. He wrote another postcard to his father and Alyson and pictured their delight at hearing from him twice in a short space of time. Might make Christian, on being excluded, sit up a bit.

He broke away from his vigil at lunch time and walked up the main street, past shops with old fashioned wooden showcases. Up one narrow street leading off it, he concentrated on the sight of an ancient tower with a cluster of trees reaching the skies from its top.

The chances were that Patricia ate her lunch indoors – rather than cycling about. He dipped into a wine store. Beneath it was a cave that housed about a thousand bottles, covered in dust and cobwebs. Not only had bottles escaped the war but, also, many of the drinkers who went before it.

These sporadic perusals of waiting and wandering

lasted for four days. On the fifth he sat, at his usual place outside the bar and Patricia rode past, looked in his direction, smiled, parked her bicycle and joined him.

Her presence did nothing to help with his inner commotion. He was as bewitched as he had been when she wasn't there. She seemed not to have registered his despair, obsession, anxiety or to be in the least bit perturbed that they hadn't met since her tumble the week before.

'I've been in Pisa. My husband, Andrea, has been giving lectures there and we stayed at the university.'

Malise ordered two cappuccinos. It was mid morning. Patricia said 'Yes. I'd love a cup of coffee. How kind. I mustn't stay long.'

'Why?'

'Why not?' She looked sharply at him. What business was it of his? He pulled himself together.

'I'm sorry. I can't think why I said that. It has been very enjoyable meeting you like this. I am, in fact, rather lonely here. Perhaps you and, er, your husband might join me for a bite one evening. I'm rather a frustrated cook to tell you the truth and I'd enjoy buying comestibles and preparing something to eat. If you don't mind seventy-nine steps, that is.'

His troubles were still with him as he devoured her beauty but he controlled his manner and captured the instant.

Patricia had already told her husband of her meeting with the handsome Englishman. She said that she must consult with him, a busy man, before accepting Malise's kind offer but, if a date could be found, might they bring their nine year old son, Antonio, along with them?'

'I know he would like to see your view and hear the bells from that level. He stays up late as Italian children do – and he speaks English and eats almost anything.'

Malise wanted her to himself, to make ludicrous love to her on a small bed after carrying her up seventy nine steps. That was not to be. Not for a while at any rate.

'Of course,' he said. 'I'd be happy to meet both your husband and your son.'

They left it that she was to telephone him when something might be fixed.

Apart from that one slip 'why,' he had not given himself away.

The dream was coming true but wrong. Half cock. He thought of his own cock as he thought, too, about food. He scrutinised shops in hopeful advance with astounding attention. It was irritating to have to provide for a child (let alone a husband) but, then, Italian children knew how to eat well compared to English ones. Sliced loaf had just come into fashion in England.

After a week and more the call came.

'You will hardly remember who I am. Patricia. We met at the bar.'

'Of course. Indeed. I'm glad you rang.'

'Please don't consider feeding us but, one evening, my husband and son would love to come with me to see your apartment. The view must be spectacular but don't the church bells keep you awake at night?'

The bells were, indeed, deafening but, since meeting her, he had barely slept – bells or not.

An evening was arranged and supper insisted on.

He strode to the local *Alimentari*. 'Elementari, dear

Watson' he said to himself, pleased with his joke. He knew little of children but planned to be boyish and boisterous with Patricia's son. A prank or two.

He had written a list. Tomato soup to start with. He cooked in his head as he shopped. After boiling four large tomatoes, he passed them through a Mouli grinder before adding chopped basil, marjoram, salt and a pinch of sugar – all with a flourish.

Then lasagne. Surely the unwelcome son ate lasagne. His fantasy, later to be played out, continued as he sprinkled parmesan, breadcrumbs, and a few small nubs of butter onto the top of the dish and baked it until brown and sizzling in a hot oven. Pudding was to be ready-made Neapolitan ice cream – bought at the end of the spree in case of melting. A carafe or two of wine – not straw-covered for fear of looking too keen to be authentic. He remembered his efforts with the Contessa.

All was bought and heaved up the side of the building in the rustic basket. Perfect. He would show the boy how the system worked and allow him to haul something up himself if necessary. He put his earlier fantasies into practice. Pinches of marjoram and salvia.

Books on Tuscany, Puccini (in reverence to the city's famous son) Volterra, Bertrand Russell and other volumes were placed where the scholarly husband of the dazzling creature was certain to see them. An old Baedeker or two filched from his father's library. A book of jokes (scherzi) he had found at the stationers – to interest the boy.

The table was tidily laid with plain paper napkins and well shone glasses.

Canapés on a dish.

20

Voices on the stairs. A child counting, crossly and in Italian – sixty-five, sixty-seven and so on. Slow and begrudging. Father encouraging. Mother encouraging. Greetings. Flourishes with canapés. Unnecessary flourishes – even Malise was awake to the fact that he overdid it.

They were all in his small sitting room. White paint. Necessities in the way of furnishing. Considering it was summer, it was chilly.

Antonio was small, dark, wiry, polite and very quiet. Patricia disconcertingly alert. More beautiful than before. Her presence unnerved Malise who gave full attention to the husband. He, like his son, was small, wiry and polite.

All went well at table – the sizzling and serving. Conversation on the sticky side but many exclamations (especially from Antonio) on the standard of the food.

Malise tried jokes – mostly about language differences – and whirled the plates to and fro to a sink, refusing all offers of help.

The only trouble was that the meal was over almost before it began. Even the ice cream was finished and the evening still very young.

Were they all going to leave by eight fifteen?

Andrea took charge and quizzed Malise about his life, his work and his reasons for living where he did. Patricia pulled a pack of cards from her bag and set up a game with her son.

Andrea began to enjoy the other's company. Malise was well educated, had learnt much about *Lucchese* brickwork. His looks were indisputably extraordinary. He managed to hint at patrician forebears. He used the word patrician in the hope that Patricia might look up from the card game – which she did.

The Mc Hips, (that was the surname, he said, modestly) were members of an ancient clan. He knew much Scottish history and Andrea found it absorbing. Wishing to sound involved in the history of Lucca, Malise embarked on another topic. 'I have heard the story of your courageous chief of police during the war. I gather he defied Mussolini and lost his life for it.'

Andrea smiled and looked serious. 'Indeed. He is a hero in particular for my family. He saved the lives of our Jewish community. Many of my relatives were rescued as a result of his brave actions. My parents, my brother and I were fortunate enough to survive in Genoa where we went to live. Our name was Levi so, we had of course, to change it. It was hard for us, as children, to remember always that our surname was now Leri. My mother made us each say it about a hundred times a morning in order to get it into our heads. Leri. Leri. Leri. I remember it clearly to this day. We were very fortunate but it wasn't easy. Much time hiding. I have always stayed with that name'

Malise emptied Andrea's ashtrays rather too frequently for the demands of hospitality and digested the unsettling fact that Patricia's husband was one from another race.

After giving the child a little talk about the church bells, he promised Antonio a demonstration with the basket and the winch – popping in the joke book and telling the boy that it was to wait for him downstairs – that it was a present to be taken home – together they reeled it down to the piazza below where it ended up beside Ruggles.

Patricia took that as a sign for them to leave. The evening was over. They thanked him and said goodbye.

'Maybe' Patricia smiled, 'Maybe you will visit us one evening. I can see that Andrea liked talking to you.'

Andrea endorsed it and, quite suddenly, asked Malise if he might be prepared to give the odd English lesson – both to him and to the boy. 'Antonio's English is good but not perfect. Patricia speaks Italian so well that we are lazy sometimes.'

There stood a chink of a link. Not that he had anticipated having to teach – but something, surely, promised. He had their address. That and their telephone number was provided by the husband.

Malise rolled up his sleeves and washed the hard, white plates; meticulously preserving remains of comestibles. He threw open windows to expel the stink of cigarettes. Sacrilege. Husband of Patricia to chain-smoke.

English lessons.

He had not reckoned on that.

In the morning he planned to buy phrase books.

Grammar. Andrea would discover how capable he was.

He was to bind his way into the family. A sort of tutor. Did tutors not, notoriously, work their ways into the beds of ladies of houses?

Certainly not a Mc Hip, but Patricia had, he told from instinct, several drops of blue blood in her. Why had she married a foreign academic? Stately homes had, surely, been open to her. Her effect on him was terrifying. It caused in him a transient feeling of faintness which came and went by the second.

He decided to let a few days pass before arranging the first lesson. Either with husband or son. The father would be the easier of the two since he wished for a lesson and the son had not looked enlivened when it had been suggested.

21

As soon as things were shipshape, he made for a *cartolleria*. All text books were, naturally, in Italian but he was unlikely to have trouble in reversing the structure.

Lessons were to be meticulously prepared. He still kept an eye open for signs of Patricia on her bicycle as he scoured the town for folders and suitable stationery. Notebooks and so on. Never before had he spent money at this speed. Never before had he fallen in love and he believed it was never to happen again in his lifetime. The iron was not hot but he had to strike.

No sign of her during that or several subsequent days. Eventually he dialed the number given to him by Andrea.

Patricia, in the loveliest and most luscious of voices, answered in Italian. 'Pronto.'

'Tutor here!' He shouted it out.

'Gosh. Yes. Andrea was a bit hopeful actually. He's terrifically busy and most often in Pisa. Thank you, though, for a great evening. You really are a master chef.'

Was that it? Was he only a chef? Were lessons no longer needed? Much spent on exercise books.

Silence. He broke it.

'What about Antonio? Might he like a modicum of tuition?' His voice grew louder still and his language more archaic.

Before the end of the conversation, however, something was arranged.

Antonio's long summer vacation had just started. Andrea spent much time in Pisa and they did not expect to go to the hills for a bit of time yet. Might Malise meet the boy in the town? Talk to him in English? *Conversazione*?

Was he about to become a child minder?

Trail a grumpy child around Lucca for hours at a time?

Unpaid, of course. To be paid by Patricia was unthinkable. He was terrified that she might suggest it. She didn't and they agreed to meet outside the cathedral on the following morning. There she was, tantalisingly so, to hand the boy over and to leave them to each other for an hour or more.

22

It was very warm. Malise, tugging at every stop within him, was determined to amuse and interest the child.

He wore, after consideration, an old linen jacket, a blue cotton shirt and army surplus trousers.

It amused him to allow the child to balance himself as he ran along a low wall that bordered a narrow canal near to the centre of the town. He bought him a multi-coloured ice cream; introduced him to the shrivelled remains of the patron saint of serving maids – having mugged up on her fanciful story. She had, he related with exaggeration in voice and manner, been stalked by an ogre (here he pretended to be an ogre) who suspected her of stealing food from his kitchen. On his orders she let fall her gathered apron and out fell a bunch of flowers. The city was brimming with myth and sensation and Malise had done all in his power to plan the walk with precision. Army surplus trousers and all. They stopped outside the orthopedic shop. An entire window was dense with dummies wearing jockstraps designed for hernia sufferers, built-up shoes, false breasts and crepe stockings under a flickering sign *'Busti e Corsetti Ortopidici.'*

Antonio was entranced by it all. Wide-eyed.

When they met Patricia at the bar where, once only, she had fallen from her bicycle, she was happy to find her son animated and asking if 'Sir' might take him walking every day. Malise, too, had enjoyed it. There was something of the schoolmaster in his make-up and, if it constituted progress towards his goal, he was more than prepared to escort the boy as often as was necessary.

He suggested that they all stop for a drink or a cup of coffee. Patricia accepted and the boy demanded another ice-cream. Malise, unmanned (or possibly the opposite) in Patricia's dazzling presence, became daring.

'Tomorrow. Why don't you join us on our round?'

She seemed surprised and pleased but refused the offer. It was clear that she delighted in her new found free time.

What did she need free time for?

Her husband was in Pisa.

The following day they repeated the ritual and, after another successful morning where the two climbed the tall tower with trees on top, they met again with Patricia at the bar. Some ice had been broken. The nine year old was much taken with Malise. The man had nothing whatsoever to do. That made a change with grown-ups who were busy from morning until night.

'Sir' was prepared to shop, change routes, allow Antonio to stroke a dog, put a lire or two into the bowl of a beggar. He became a Galahad in the child's eyes.

23

For several days they kept to the same routine – joining Patricia for a drink in the Piazza when the touring round was over. They boy was attentive to Malise who, flaunting boyish suppleness, showed him how to make paper aeroplanes and raced him round the ramparts. Patricia beamed upon him, her sparkling eyes looking into his.

'What luck that we met. Antonio has seldom enjoyed himself more. Andrea and I are both so busy.'

'What makes you busy?'

He had her attention. Never, ever had he been close to such loveliness.

She said 'I work at the art school. Only part time. Otherwise I paint.'

Her lips were thick and full. Her son put his arms around her and kissed both her cheeks. Lucky boy.

At the start of the enterprise Andrea had suggested that his son call Malise 'Sir.'

On that day Antonio, after kissing his mother, leaned

towards Malise and said 'Sir. Why do you not come with us to our holiday house?' Patricia smiled. Malise lived in purgatory as he waited for her reaction.

'That's a nice idea darling.' – talking to her boy – 'but you know we can't have guests there.' She turned to Malise and smiled again – yet more warmly.

'We do have a little holiday house up in the Pisan hills. Not far from here. It's heaven but not fit for visitors.'

She went on, still smiling, to explain that it was really barely more than a ruin. No plumbing, no electricity, a cooker with need of a gas bombola. Just a small beauty spot with a stream. A wood. Kingfishers, wild boar, flowers, birds, bats and red squirrels. Cuckoos sang in spring and summer.

It was one o'clock and Malise suggested 'a spot of lunch in a *trattoria* perhaps?'

'Yes. Si. Si' Antonio was overjoyed.

At lunch in a dark *trattoria*, as Antonio tucked in to a heap of spaghetti, Patricia told Malise more. They each drank a glass of pale white wine. Pale, almost, as water.

24

After lunch, Malise suggested they walk (Patricia leaving her bicycle where it was parked) to the *piazza* below his apartment. He wanted Antonio to see his car for it had been half-hidden behind a van on the evening when he had visited with his parents.

'He's called 'Ruggles' Malise explained as the boy fingered dark blue body work and asked for a ride.

'Another time' he said. Good idea to ration out treats.

'The key is up all those stairs and I, for one, have had enough walking for today, my lad.'

'Why is he called 'Ruggles'?'

Malise looked mysteriously at Patricia and said 'Thereby hangs a tale.'

He found it fitting that she suspect he had some sort of a past.

Antonio, entranced, wheeled towards his mother.

'Why can't Sir drive it to the *Casetta*? It can stay at the bottom of the hill where Papa leaves his car.'

Ruggles was muscelling in on the act. Bringing good fortune.

'Young man. Tell me where to find you and I'll call by – ready with my hammock. Do you have a tree or two?'

'Lots and lots and lots of trees.'

Fortunate he had thought to buy a hammock before setting out on his travels.

By the time they parted, Malise had set out a scheme whereby, sometime during the family's holiday in the hills, he would pay them a visit in 'Ruggles' – and looked forward to roping his hammock between two of their trees.

He was not certain if Patricia entirely approved of the idea but Antonio was adamant.

They were gone but, in a very few days, he planned to follow them. He planned, too, that the boy should call him 'Captain.' After all, he was one. It didn't sound very glamorous in England but, in Italy – 'Capitano.'

25

A visit to the public post office was horribly overdue and Malise walked there grudgingly, but at a smart pace.

Sure enough a large and floppy envelope had waited there for many weeks. The letter came from Christian and was written on lined paper.

'Dear Malise. I write to ask after you (and Ruggles, too, of course)

Daddy and Alyson were pleased with your cards but not much the wiser. Not too good here I'm afraid. I'm sorry to have to tell you that Daddy's in poor shape. Angina they say. He falls a lot and looks ancient. Of course he was old when we were born (especially me). I know that Alyson is pretty worried. The farm's not in good nick either. Alyson keeps reminding me that it all now belongs to you. I daresay you won't turf us out if anything happens to Daddy but might you be able to give us an idea of future plans? I, for one, am loving being back in the choir and, guess what? I've been made senior scout. Needless to say,

Daddy would welcome a visit from you. That is to say, if you can spare the time.'

The letter went on to tell of the poor condition of farm machinery. Roof tiles damp here and there. No trace of affection from his brother.

Malise could, of course, not spare time to visit Hertfordshire just then but replied, by letter that evening, that before long he was certain to present himself. What if Christian managed to usurp him? Probably not legally possible at this late stage.

Following days were taken up with preparation for the drive in Ruggles to Patricia's country hideaway. Not far from Lucca. Barely twenty kilometres. Funny to have a country retreat so near to the city – but Italians always made a habit of travelling short distances to their hideaways. He decided, although it was a wrench for him, to leave his Teddy bear behind. He didn't want Antonio asking questions.

He made a pile of boyish objects – likely to be useful and to impress. Hammock. Torch. Matches. Knife. Rope. Candles. A stretch of tarpaulin. Spirit lamp. He would set up a camp – somewhere in the woods that Antonio had talked to him about. Foodstuffs. Non perishables. They were heaped in a corner of the apartment. Several basket loads to raise and lower.

26

Off he set, through arches under the city walls, and off towards the hills. Ruggles bulged with props.

His person, his overall frame, looked pretty good, Malise decided, as he guided the Lagonda through ribbons of village development that had sprung up, helter-skelter, since the war.

Bars, bikes, neon signs. He smiled at quaintness as he read a placard advertising 'Warm Dogs.' A new and distorted influence from America. A sure party punch line.

He stopped at a *rotisseria* where he bought grilled chicken wings, salami slices and delicacies.

Then, past olives, vines, plane trees, presses, pizzerias, bridges and dirty ditches. Italian ditches were, on the whole, murky and awash with dead rats. He blanked out the war years – apart from remembering that he was a Captain. A popular figure in and among brave people of the resistance.

It was perplexing – trying to translate the instructions

of a nine year old. Up, round, under, rutted lanes, broken buildings, ditches, streams, shaky telegraph poles. A small village where he stopped at a shop and asked for the whereabouts of an English family.

When he knew he was near his destination, he left his precious car near by a wrecked barn and walked up a hill, carrying little equipment. It would not do to look as if he planned to settle. Might the husband be there?

The small house was built into a hill and encircled by pine woods. All around were streams, olive trees and birds – in spite, he noted, of the mercilessness of the hunters who were famous for shooting at every bumble bee. Paths were littered with empty cartridges.

She was there, standing on a rough terrace in a pale muslin frock. Hair held back by a pink ribbon. Beside her stood Antonio who squealed in delight and left her side. 'Sir. Sir. Will you take me for an adventure? Is your car here?'

Malise stood firm and tall, puffing out his rib cage. 'Hello. I've traced you. What a place!'

Patricia, puzzled, asked how he had found them. They were very isolated. No telephone. No actual address. He answered that Antonio had been accurate in his instructions but that he had, also, asked one or two of the locals for 'Inglese' in the neighbourhood.

'You are popular round here. They knew you well at the village shop.'

It was after midday and Patricia asked him to stay and join them for lunch. He planned on staying a good deal longer than a mere lunch hour but said 'Thank you kindly. Delighted to do so,' as he pulled at his imaginary forelock.

A stone table stood beside the house. It was sheltered from the sun by a vine and on it sat a tray covered in fig leaves and piled high with peaches.

Patricia carried a plateful of rissoles and a tomato salad from the kitchen, only two paces away, and asked Antonio to fill a jug with clear, cold water from a nearby spring.

'I hope there will be enough' she said 'I barely eat at all when Andrea is in Pisa – and we hadn't catered for company had we Antonio?'

Malise thought her a little confused and feared that he, too, showed what his stepmother would have called 'lack of finish.'

He spoke jerkily as he looked to the table and muttered 'a rissole, fruit and salad. All anyone could wish for.'

It wasn't, of course, all that he wished for but, a rissole, fruit and salad passed muster for the time being.

Antonio returned with spring water and began, at once, to pester and also to diffuse the awkwardness. It wasn't quite the moment to begin on the 'Capitano' business, so he allowed the boy to continue with cries of 'Sir. Sir. Did you bring your hammock? I have found two trees where it can go.'

Three kitchen chairs were pulled up to the stone table and, as they ate, the discomfort started to dwindle. Patricia was proud of her rustic haven and pleased to show it off to an Englishman. Her Italian friends found it weird and inconvenient.

Malise provided a rewarding willingness to exclaim on the splendour around them and asked, with keenness, how she had ever come by such an enchanted spot.

He told her that he had planned to drive on to Volterra

that day; had research to do there. It had been obvious from Antonio's instructions that they lay, indeed, on the route to that city. The detour he made appeared convincing and Patricia relaxed as he gave way to Antonio's persuasions.

A spindly boy, of an age with Antonio, appeared from the terrace below. A date had been made for the children to spend the rest of the day together. Antonio raced towards the visiting boy and cried 'A friend of Mamma's,' pointing to Malise, 'Sir here – has a car – below. A fantastic car. We will make him take us to it.' The visiting boy looked startled and admitted to having wondered at the sight of Ruggles – never guessing that he was to meet the owner.

Patricia melted. This handsome newcomer had captured the heart of her only child. She had reading and painting to do as well as many an odd job to see to around the house. Allow Antonio to be amused and entertained. Let her off the hook. She doted on her son but doted, too, on free time.

Malise, Antonio and the extra boy walked down the track that lay between a ditch and a precipice – to the dilapidated barn beside which the Lagonda was parked.

'Now boys!' he said, attempting playfulness, 'If I give you a ride in Ruggles, I shall expect you to call me Capitano.' He spoke in faulty Italian with appeals to Antonio to translate for the visitor.

Before taking a ride, they had to empty the back of the car – the carrying orchestrated by Malise. All objects were stacked in the ruin of a barn on the step of which a toad squatted.

The boys talked feverishly in both languages – the one

translating for the other.

'Capitano. Will you come swimming with us? In the stream. We aren't allowed to unless grown-ups are with us.'

Malise said 'Yes' to everything as they cleared Ruggles of equipment.

'First a spin, then a swim.' Malise was near to being in his element although anxiety concerning his desires prevented him from tasting the joys of total delight.

The boys took it in turn to sit in the back. Windows down and waving. They insisted on stopping outside the village shop where there was always an audience on its doorstep. Then they drove up a long and winding track, but the young passengers soon began to tire for there were no people, on that deserted route, to admire them in Ruggles. They urged Malise to return. It was time for a swim. Malise had, he remembered, packed a pair of bathing trunks in among his bulging bags.

Back at the barn where his stuff awaited him, Malise instructed Antonio and his friend – 'Run up the hill boys. Tell Mamma that you have talked me into setting up a camp in her wood tonight. Tell her that you will all, your friend too of course, be welcome to come and sup with me tonight. To partake of a bosky meal.'

'By the way,' he asked 'does your Papa come home today? Just so that I have an idea of how many to provide for.'

'Papa never comes until Saturdays. He comes only for one or two nights and sometimes only in the day time.'

It was a Monday.

'Supper for three then. In the wood on the other side of the stream from your house. Beside an old shed.'

Off they scampered, bursting with delight, to take the news to Patricia who painted at the stone table.

Three times Malise walked, each time carrying a heavy load, to the spot he had marked down for his camp – a small stretch of flat terrace beside a collapsing shed.

He worried as he imagined Antonio breaking the news to his mother and hastened to sort out his belongings. He craved the sight of her in her muslin frock and pink bow.

He had just dumped his last load, tent included, onto the grass when the boys reappeared. They were ready to swim and Antonio carried a note from his mother. First letter ever from Patricia. His hand trembled as he read the scrawled lines. 'Antonio tells me that you are to camp here tonight – and that you have invited us to 'sup' with you. He was not sure what you meant by 'sup' but I guess that you are asking us to eat with you this evening? It is kind of you. Luigi, Antonio's friend, can't stop. His mother wants him back. So, the two of us will find your hideaway with no trouble. Early please as I don't like to keep my boy up late. Andrea will not be back today I fear. Sometimes, though, in Antonio's holidays, he can be flexible. Later I shall go down to the Posto Publico to find a message from him. Our only form of communication here. Meanwhile I gather you are going to supervise the boys as they swim. It is extremely kind of you.'

He hid the letter in his sleeping bag. First memento.

Malise shuddered at the likelihood of Andrea's flexibility.

27

He stood tall, pectorals outstanding, in shallow water as the boys jumped and splashed. It was not deep enough to swim in. There was always a chance that Patricia might, at the very least, come to watch.

He kept up an act of boyish playfulness – just in case. At one moment the children seemed to tire of paddling. Malise climbed out of the water and bade them watch him stand on his head. He told them to count to see if he was still upside down when they got to a hundred. He was. Just, although mauve in colour. But no Patricia to witness the feat. Not without effort, he kept up his pranks until he heard her summon the boys in for tea – as she called their afternoon snack. No more than her voice. No sight of the pink ribbon. The muslin dress. The body beneath it.

Malise threw all his strength into preparation. He spread a length of tarpaulin on top of the stretch of flattened grass and balanced a bread board on a handy plank of wood. Setting out several candles in glass jars, he looked about for suitable places in which to place the quantity of spirales he had brought along with him. These were circles of green repellent material – attached to metal bases – holders, ready to be lit with a match and to smoulder for hour after hour – keeping mosquitoes at a distance. He was pleased to have thought of that, not wishing to itch or to swell on any part of his body. Nor did he wish itching or swelling on any part of Patricia's body.

He had brought, too, plastic mugs, plates, containers and an oil lamp, cushions – even a bread knife. He did not peg the tent for he planned to sleep in his hammock and, also, felt that the erecting of a tent might give his stay the impression of semi-permanence. Tact was required. And skill.

The venue for the 'sup' was ready and pretty well perfect by the time Patricia and Antonio walked down the path to join him.

'Hi.' His voice abnormally loud again.

'I should not really say welcome when this is your home.'

'Maybe not.' Patricia answered in a near-to-formal manner but Antonio spoke, in a rush and in Italian to his mother. He extolled the wonders of the 'Capitano' – his car, his head-standing exploits, the many marvels of the man until the boy's mother relaxed and appeared to be at ease. They settled and ate and talked until it darkened and fire flies flicked about. Mosquitos were deterred by the smouldering spirales. Malise served contentedly and with, once again, a great many flourishes. Patricia gave the impression of easing, letting go, enjoying herself. It was good to hear her beauty spot extolled and marvelled at. She began to respond to his queries and described her moment of coming upon the place four years earlier.

They had explored (Andrea, herself and Antonio – then three years old) the area one autumn day. They had looked for blackberries and enjoyed a day away from the city. A sly local fellow had joined them on the hillside, pointed to the collapsing house and offered it for sale. That and a good number of surrounding hectares at a very low price.

Her voice.

Antonio amused himself fiddling with candles and spirales. Patricia lay back on a cushion and said 'Oh god! That guitarist again.' Music, from a distance and badly played, followed their ears. Patricia went on 'Poor Andrea. He can't bear that noise; goes half mad when it starts up – but – well. I rather like it. Company perhaps.'

Malise was on the alert. 'Company? Was she lonely?

When and how was he to suggest that he stayed longer on her land?

Antonio was drowsy and Patricia said that they must be off.

Tomorrow? Was he going on to Volterra in the morning she asked. If so she thanked him for an excellent 'sup' and for having been so very good to Antonio and his friend. 'Perhaps, on your way back, you might like to call by. Andrea, if he is with us, would be pleased to see you again. Headway? He gave no firm answer but, when they had gone, cleared up, snuffed candles, packed food in plastic bags and lodged them under stones beside the stream. Waste not want not, as he had been taught at the farm in Hertfordshire.

Patricia was only a few hundred yards from where he hooked his hammock. She was there in her unlit house. He crept near to it and watched the beam of a torch through an upper window as she shone herself to bed.

'To bed. To bed. To bed' he sang as he rocked, uncontrollably, in his hammock.

28

He was bitten by mosquitoes and prevented from sleeping by the amateur guitarist – as well as by his own inner torments.

After dropping off for an hour or two he was woken by the call of a late summer cuckoo and a throng of black-caps that flurried in a cluster of tall trees near to sturdy ones onto which he'd hooked his hammock.

Gypsies slunk by carrying bundles of, presumably, Patricia's logs. He was tempted to confront them. Take up cudgels on her behalf. Knight in armour.

It was five thirty in the morning. Malise had no idea what to do next but the conquest of Patricia was the thing that must be achieved. Strategy was required. It was all very well to be male companion and mentor to Antonio in the absence of the boy's father – but what when Andrea returned?

It was not an easy job to extricate himself from the hammock and his skin was lined with the pattern of rope.

He washed in the stream and felt that his feet were a long way from his head and that his mouth had gone very dry. All a result of vacillating moments.

Later, and after a long walk of exploration through bracken, brambles, ferns, trees and streams, he sat on the tarpaulin to eat fruit and a stale roll.

Patricia visited him alone. She wore a different dress and a blue bow, rather than the pink one of the day before, held back her shimmering, dark hair.

'Thank you for our delicious supper.'

'Pleasure Ma'am.' He sprang up.

'How was your night in the hammock?'

'Excellent. Never slept better.'

'Are you off to Volterra?'

'I thought. Yes. I'll push off there sometime today.'

He never knew what took place as those short sentences had been exchanged but, at some point, he realised that Patricia asked him to stay put for a while.

For further days.

'Antonio has begged me to persuade you to stay in your camp for more of his holidays.'

'Did you need to be begged?'

He feared that he had overstepped the mark. If he overstepped, Patricia side-stepped and gave him her hand.

A whisper of delight passed between them; the message of a magic touch. A flutter, a flush, a fuzziness. Whatever it wasn't – it was an immodest thing.

Patricia, she told him within seconds, had been holding back – had sheltered behind her son and her marriage. She told him that she would return to her house, tell Antonio to help Malise pitch his tent before, in peculiar mood, tripping down to the *Posto Publico* to hear news of and to send news to her husband, Andrea. The world, for her, moved oddly as though she were being led by an ominous fatality.

29

He was glad that he had cleaned his teeth after eating the stale roll and before kissing Patricia's lips. Fortunate.

Very soon, Antonio was there, helping to erect the tent and rejoicing that the Capitano planned to stay on.

Patricia returned, on light feet, from the village where she had exchanged handwritten (by Rosina, the postmistress) messages with Andrea who was not able to join them for several more days. He was sad not to be as flexible as he often was during school holidays but workload in Pisa, where he stayed at the university, was unusually heavy. He missed them both and had much hoped to surprise them,

Malise asked Antonio 'Your friend. The one who was here yesterday. Do you sometimes go and play with him at his house?'

'Not often. It's more fun exploring here. Especially now you have the camp and Ruggles.'

That was bad news.

'It might be nice for them to feel that they can return your hospitality.'

Antonio was puzzled and did not answer. Patricia, flummoxed, did duty by her son.

'Oh. That's OK. He's an only child and his mother works. Not easy for them.'

Malise was downcast but knew that his only hope was to pretend to make the best of things. He was, otherwise, wholly elated and knew that, before long, he was certain to get Patricia to himself. That one kiss told him that she responded energetically to his passion.

He had no way of seeing his reflection. No portable looking glass. If only he could confirm that he was likely, still, to be taken for an effigy; a god of masculine beauty. It was necessary to rely on faith and confidence.

They were not to be alone together until after it was dark. The three of them 'supped' at the stone table outside Patricia's rickety kitchen. Candles, spirales, pasta, peaches. Tartlets from the village shop. More fire flies. Bats twirled above them. Malise broke the party up.

'Well. *Grazie* to both of you. I'm off to my tent. Good morrow to you both.' He made a stiff bow.

Later, an hour or so later, when Antonio had gone to sleep, Patricia went, armed with pillows and other comforts, to join Malise in his tent.

Together they fell onto a thin mattress through which twigs prickled. They behaved together in a furious fashion. In a fashion hitherto untried by either.

Malise, for a second or two, remembered Dawn, his kilt and his dead mother. But not for long.

Eagerness, sex, disregard for all but their senses, led

them through a great part of the night. The neighbouring guitarist made no impression whatsoever on either of the pulsating pair.

Patricia slipped back to her bedroom and Malise, by the light of a strong torch, bathed in the cold stream.

He did not return, for the remainder of the night, to the hammock but drifted away in gratification on a pillow provided by Patricia.

The need to entertain Antonio during the day was frustrating but made tolerable by the celestial anticipation of nights ahead.

30

It was Wednesday and another message from the *Posto Publico* announced that Andrea was to arrive by car on Friday evening. Patricia had no car of her own and relied on her feet when unable to ride her bicycle on rough and hilly ground. Lucky the village shop was within walking distance.

Malise, finding it impossible to be with Patricia on her own during the day whilst she attended to her son, took Ruggles for a spin or two. This was much to the disappointment of Antonio and Malise had to spend patient times explaining about work taking him away for hours at a time.

On one of the days, he did drive to Volterra – partly in order to send a postcard to his father and to show that Etruscan studies still absorbed him and made it hard for him to return to the farm yet awhile.

He greatly liked Volterra but, with the newly discovered rapture of contact with Patricia's body, there was little likelihood of his moving to live there.

Lucca, in term time, was to be an unassailable haven. Andrea in Pisa, Antonio at school all day and blissful antics at the top of the seventy-nine steps.

With feverish fingers, twitching toes and throbbing member, no longer did he view himself as a desiccated loner. His stiffness evaporated. He decided not to try to make any more stately jokes.

In Volterra, he ate frugally at a *trattoria* on a narrow pavement beside a shop that sold alabaster objects formed to look like different fruits. They were convincingly set out as though at a greengrocer's store. He bought an alabaster peach for Patricia. Tempted by a pear as well but allowed caution to dominate.

He drove back to his camp in the evening after sending the postcard. Three more Andrea-free nights. Celestial squirming on the thin mattress. Body in a spasm. He was nearly forty and, apart from preliminary forages, such rapture had never crossed his path. His mother's teaching, 'All Things Bright and Beautiful' on his childhood bedroom wall, Alyson's righteousness, Christian's adoration of him – dissolved as if they had been nothing at all. The agitation in him almost amounted to a divine form of terror.

On the way back he pulled Ruggles to a halt and shopped for supper. Non-stop spending.

Partricia and Antonio were scheduled to join them to 'sup' beside his tent. After Antonio's bed time, Patricia would return to him for more throbbing, more thunderous power from within him. Fireflies, frogs croaking, tent shaking. A family of wild boar tramping past. An enchanted place.

The days passed.

Friday was upon them and the arrival of Andrea prepared for. The atmosphere altered. Patricia became anxious and a little distant. Antonio was excited.

Malise was proud to find himself badly ruffled by spasms of exaltation and agony that succeeded each other by the hour. No longer self-sufficient and dignified as he had once believed himself to be.

Andrea arrived. Neat, smiling, friendly – but with firm gravity of face – and chain-smoking. He and his wife appeared easy together. Easy and affectionate. It was understood that Malise join them for meals at the stone table by the crumbling house.

He heard them (and saw them if he strained) making preparations. Ashtrays for Andrea. Bottles of respectable wine. Grapes. Fennel salad. Coloured napkins.

The two men met for the second time in their lives. It was the first time since Malise had become the lover of the other's wife.

'What a marvellous place you have here.'

'I am happy that you find it like that. It was a gesture towards my English wife. She loves the countryside. We live very tidy in an apartment just outside the Lucca walls and this is her freedom.'

31

Supper, smoke and candles, went well. Andrea asked Antonio many questions about their activities during his absence. Antonio regaled his father with stories of Ruggles, bathing, head-standing, the hammock – 'sups' beside the tent.

The lean and immaculately dressed Andrea was amused and interested. Malise did not follow the language well but made himself useful – taking plates in and out and trying to kiss Patricia when he found her scraping a bowl in the kitchen. She was awkward and flushed. It was all terrible.

When the time came for Antonio to go to bed, Patricia took him upstairs and read to him by gas light as the two men lingered over wine and remains of supper.

Andrea spoke English fluently but without competence.

'Tell me more of you' he asked with great good manners and no suspicion.

'We liked very much to meet you when we came to your beautiful apartment. I ask you again. What brings you to our city of Lucca?'

Malise answered, giving some attention to bricks but shirking detail. Andrea was a professor and it might have been hard for Malise not to appear spurious or give himself away.

Andrea probably knew more about Etruscan history than he did and Malise put their language barrier to good use as the other smoked many cigarettes and spoke sadly of the war years and, again, of his families escape from the cruelty of Mussolini. Malise showed tender sympathy as he re-registered how far Patricia had strayed from her, unmistakably, noble English origins. Andrea thanked Malise for his kindness to Patricia and Antonio during his absences but promised that, for the remainder of the holidays, he was to spend more time with them.

'It is hard for my English wife to be alone with only a child for company.'

Before Patricia had finished reading to Antonio in his bedroom, Malise went to his patch and decided that, in the morning, he would pack Ruggles with his possessions, including tent and hammock, and head back for Lucca.

Present restraints imposed on him by the situation were intolerable. There were many weeks left before term started when the family were ready to return to their city life. Andrea driving each day to Pisa and his studies.

At breakfast he followed Patricia into the kitchen and, with misery scratched all over his face, explained that he had need to disappear. Too near and far too far. He also slipped a note into her hand as she brewed coffee. Her men folk were outside at the stone table. The note gave her his address in case she had not registered the exact number of his apartment. She handed him a scrap of paper too. On it were written the details of somewhere that he would find her. In the village. A friend who was to be trusted. An Englishwoman married to an Italian electrician.

With many a complicated pang, he drove to Lucca and to the *Posto Publico* where he was handed another letter from Christian. It was not pitiful or at all affectionate but urged him to return if only for a short while.

'Daddy is very weak and Alyson not coping well. There is business to be seen to and, I gather, you are to be in charge. I always felt things should be equally divided between us but – there we go!'

32

Having written a few lines of love and further explanation to Patricia, Malise turned a large key after closing his apartment door. He then locked Ruggles and left it in the courtyard before planning to leave by train for Pisa airport. After a second's thought, he decided to hide the car key in the apartment. Up he went again, unlocked the door, entered and slid the ignition key under an ancient brick.

He knew that the answer lay in his returning to the farm and staying there until term began in Lucca. He must contain himself until then. There were many weary weeks to be killed. Denial.

Down the steps again. From Pisa he flew to London. Then he took a train from Liverpool Street to the old familiar station where he was met by an enigmatic Christian in 'my old banger.'

Things were bad at the farm. The father was fragile, walked with two sticks and barely spoke. He showed pleasure with a toothy smile when he saw Malise but said nothing.

Alyson, also walking with two sticks, told, before he had been more than minutes in the house, interminable tales of woe.

Malise was still expected to share a room with Christian. Neither man queried that. His Teddy bear had also travelled back from Lucca – so a worn and weary-eyed Teddy lay on each bed as they had done in the old days when the boys' mother read them tracts.

Household duties had become Christian's responsibility, shopping, cooking, firewood. A woman came in from the village to clean but was, according to Christian 'wather hawum-scawum' and stole things.

In the bedroom, Christian asked, with some hostility about the 'Etwuscans', but drew little reward.

One evening, however, as they lay in their single beds, Malise was overcome by an urge to confide. Christian was the only ear available to him as he writhed and craved Patricia's body.

'Christian' he asked as he lay in the dark facing his brother's bed. 'Have you ever been in love?'

Christian, astounded by this bolt from the blue, took time to answer.

After a short while, however, he said 'No, Malise. I don't think so. I've lost my heart to one or two of the scouts and choir boys – lovely lads, but nothing much more.'

Malise was trembling and not himself. 'I have Christian. I know what it is.'

The words left him as shots from a rifle. One after another. He told his brother of the bicycle tumble; the tracking down, nights in the tent. Startling details. Arrival of the husband. Sore heart. Aching limbs. Terror of loss.

Never before had he bared himself to a living soul. With Patricia he had been too busy huffing and puffing for much speech. Detailed though his revelations were, Malise failed to mention Andrea's Jewish origins. They didn't quite fit with the Italian picture he wanted to paint.

Christian, although near to uncomprehending, gloated over the power he now held. Unsympathetic confidante. Heart intact, he purred as he slept.

Appearing not to remember his outpourings to his brother, Malise spent some time, most days, with his father who did barely more than nod – and with Alyson who poured out lists of lamentations and repeatedly told him that it was unpleasant to live to an old age.

One morning she handed over a damp pile of letters addressed to him.

'They have been here for some while dear but it didn't seem safe to forward them to that funny Box number. Fortunate I didn't since you are now here.'

Some were merely formal – from tailors and shoemakers, a card from the debutante he had danced with at The Hyde Park Hotel to tell him that she was getting married.

One came from Mr Scarlatti of schoolboy days.

'I write with little expectation of a reply. I am sad to have lost touch with you and your fellow pupils but pin my hopes on the chance that you can still be contacted at this address. You are, by now, I imagine, a happily married man with a large and thriving family. I have been unfortunate in that, soon after retiring, I fell victim to an arthritic complaint and now live in a care home. The people are kind but time hangs heavy on my hands and it would give me untold pleasure to hear how you fared after the atrocious war. Correspondence with your old school has led me to believe that you survived it and distinguished yourself. As you know, I had high hopes for you and have every reason to believe that they have been fulfilled. Yours in hope of a reply. J.Scarlatti.'

'PS I do not seek pity but it is impossible for me to exaggerate the wretched state to which I have been reduced and the heartache that I cannot subdue. We have, perhaps, all lost something in the pain of war but, with the collapse of my health, no one has lost what I have lost – all early hopes and many of them, my boy, were for you. JS.'

Malise felt sorry for Mr Scarlatti in his care home but knew that no good would become of renewing their friendship – if that was what it had been. He would send him a card, later on, from Italy. Picture of an Etruscan urn.

The weather was fine and, after sessions with his father, he usually walked around the garden as he pictured Patricia, possibly on her bike. Wished he was her bike. Lucky bike.

He was shocked by the ramshackle condition of the garden. Overgrown and dismal. Seats broken and unpainted. Branches fallen helter-skelter. He decided to tackle it in a manly fashion. Christian was gloating and much taken up with scouts, choir and village pursuits. 'A bit of do-gooding' he would say, smugly, as he slipped from the house.

As well as trying to sort out business matters and to establish his ownership of the no-longer-desirable property, he spent hours, mostly lusting, in the garden.

How rewarding it would have been were Patricia there to witness the tackling of his tasks.

After a few false starts, he wrote to her. He wanted her to know how well he did but wanted, too, to show light heartedness. Feared that complaints might not show as manly. Several drafts. Different paper, nibs, headings, inks, endearments.

It ended up as follows.

'My angel.

I miss you non-stop but have spent an inordinate amount of time coping with the almost hopelessly overgrown shrubbery at the end of the garden here. Last winter's mild weather and abundant rain gave the shrubs a chance to unite into a single wall of vegetation, cleverly threaded with bramble to repel attack (holly too). Plainly a plot had been hatched by them! But I fought back, crawling in beneath them with a bushman's saw, and the cost of much blood, and laid the enemy low. Then, of course, they all had to be cut up, wheel-barrowed away and burnt. And then I had to dig up the roots, though often frustrated by tap-roots. On top of that I have been re-glazing half of the green house, also clearing out a century's deposit of wood, iron, glass, old pig feeders, useless tools etc from the large carpenter's loft and taking unusable items to the dump. I won't go on with the litany! There was a good deal of satisfaction in getting all this done, but, really, I overworked and now have to draw in my belt by two notches to keep my trousers up.'

He wanted her to remember his trousers and to picture him in masculine mode.

He also mentioned that he was planning to write his autobiography as he had a tale or two to tell. Interesting man behind the handsome face. He sent his regards to

Andrea and Antonio, added a great many words of adoration, sealed the letter up and walked in military strides to the village post office where he basked in the slight stir he caused by asking for a foreign stamp. Weeks still to go. He eyed the telephone kiosk. If he could but hear her voice. But he had no number. Or, rather, she had no telephone in her woodland retreat.

33

As well as composing his letter to Patricia (which took several days), passing time in the garden, as described in the composition, talking to his father, his stepmother, and occasionally and formally with his brother (but never referring to his foolish nocturnal outpouring), Malise held conferences with a local solicitor. It was the moment to put matters in place. There were several weeks to go before Antonio's school term began and, if matters were not settled by then, it would be a case of dividing his time between Lucca and the Hertfordshire farm house until they were.

Together with the solicitor, mutterings from Christian, silence from the father and lamentations from Alyson, it was decided that the old pair move to a care home in the next village but one. It was inopportunely known as 'The Grid.' The name had been much criticised in the neighbourhood when first the institution opened, but the place had been converted from old farm buildings and the main house stood on the site of a long-disused cattle grid. Notwithstanding opposition it continued to be called 'The Grid' and the staff were known to be kind.

Alyson was resigned. She already knew three dwellers there, all widows, and she hoped to be included in their bridge circle although her game was rusty.

The farmhouse was to be let with arrangement for Christian to keep three rooms at the back. One of these was to be their shared bedroom so that Malise would always have somewhere to sleep on his visits to the old place.

'As you know Christian.' He spoke with less certainty than in the past – now that Christian was party to his secret. 'I may be away a great deal. This place does belong to me but I am happy to let you stay on for the time being. If, when I return from time to time, I shall put up a bed in the downstairs room. It's high time we had rooms of our own.' With Patricia in mind, he was a grown man.

All this needed much sorting and constant argument – largely over which pieces of furniture Alyson wished to take with her to The Grid.

An anxious Malise knew that many days were likely to be needed for a letter to travel to the Pisan hills where Patricia was to be handed it by her conspiratorial neighbour.

He wrote several similar ones – doubly reminding her of his manliness, his sense of duty and the notch in his trousers.

It was at least a fortnight before a reply came. Remembering, with extraordinary vividness, her writing from the brief note she had handed him and knowing that no other letter was likely to come for him with an Italian stamp attached, his hands trembled as he opened it. To his infinite but momentary joy, it contained more than just a line or two. His infinite joy departed but the trembling continued as he read on.

'Dear Malise. I have now had three letters from you, all posted in England, and thank you for all of them BUT, I fear, they must now stop.'

Lead entered his body.

'The days you spent here were wonderful but I was, and I'm sorry to say this, in cloud cuckoo land. I was a little starved of 'Englishness' and you were more than brilliant with Antonio. Thank you for that and for our unreal time together.

No more but best wishes for your great tasks. I will endeavour to take a different route when I bicycle through Lucca – until I know you are no longer living there for I hate the idea of hurting you further. I will make enquiries at the bar. Yours in deep regret for any misunderstandings. Patricia.'

Had his letters in some way 'put her off'?

He had taken much trouble over them. Even reminded her of his trousers. It was unimaginable. All his thoughts were centred around her. Not that he wanted Andrea to leave her. God forbid! The last thing he needed was to find himself supporting a wife on his meagre income – possibly a child too – if he turned out to constitute the guilty party in a divorce.

He had no idea what to do next or how to handle his desires which were still exceedingly strong.

Surely, he would find her on her bicycle. There were not

that many cycling routes through the ancient city. Were he to track her down, then there was every chance that, upon sighting him, (particularly with the two tightened notches) she would melt in a moment.

He wrote again.

'My very dearest Patricia. Whoa there! Your letter landed me with a bomb shell. I can only believe that you have been struck by pangs of conscience. I respect you for that. You have a delightful husband and I have no wish to hold myself responsible for breaking up a happy family such as yours. However, I don't see why we may not continue to meet – when it suits your domestic life of course – and continue to pursue the wonders that we were able to provide for each other. '

Many screech marks later, he finished the letter by telling her more of his self-sacrificing experiences.

He stalked off again to the post office, pleased with the epistle. Pleased, too, that he hadn't humbled himself. Mc Hips were a proud people.

'.

34

It was aggravating to see Christian behaving in a contented fashion. He drove in and out of the gate in his 'old banger' and enjoyed moving furniture around in preparation for the great changes in their household. Malise began to have doubts as to what these changes were in aid of – apart from the advantage of preserving his property for the future with Christian there to look after things and an income for letting out most of the house. That income was needed for upkeep – garden and maintenance. His father's own money was to pay for what was left of the old couples' lives at The Grid.

He read and re-read Patricia's letter. What particularly flabbergasted him was her writing of avoiding him in Lucca. Not even a last meeting. He wondered if Antonio had suspected anything on the occasions when his mother left him alone in an unlit house to spend euphoric hours on the prickly mattress.

What he refused to accept was that his charms had

SUSANNA JOHNSTON

faded in her mind.

He did not hear from her again.

Weeks passed.

School term, in Italy, had begun. It irked him that he still paid rent, albeit very little, for the apartment high up among the church bells.

Nights with Christian were a torment. His brother snored loudly and contentedly – no demons crippling his heart.

They were no longer on speaking terms but each man had a Teddy bear at his side. The floor was covered in the same drear linoleum that had provided a base for their early togetherness.

Malise's efforts to sleep were riddled with pain and anxiety. He, who had deemed himself equal to any crisis, was now helpless.

He woke early each morning.

One morning in particular.

Christian was still breathing like a grampus and Malise noticed that his own slippers were not beside his bed as usual although his brother's were in place. He had, it transpired, left them in the bathroom. Out of character.

He also began to worry that he had misplaced deeds of the house and other papers left by the solicitor for him to re-read.

He did find the papers and his confidence was partially restored. These slight aberrations, he supposed, were the direct result of shock.

One evening there was a kerfuffle. Alyson mislaid her pills. The ones that were normally propped up beside the clock on the mantelpiece. Malise did not remember throwing them into a dustbin and the mystery was never fully resolved although he had a dim inkling of his own responsibility concerning the drama. He had always despised medication. New prescriptions had to be sent for and Alyson was fretful and accusatory.

Christian's disenchantment with him had not taken root until after the war and it came to him that, apart from that, he had never been rejected; not by Mr Scarlatti, Dawn, debutantes, foreign lasses. Not by Patricia – until now. Something like pandemonium overtook him; deep uncertainty; unhappiness, fear and acute panic. His hands shook and his feet tightened into cramp. Sometimes he fed recklessly on illusions as he reeled emotionally about. Blood pounded through his veins. Hot and cold. Rejection petrified him.

Antonio must have snooped. Reported matters to his father. His father was a smoker; neurotic. A showdown had followed and he, Malise, had not been there to comfort Patricia. It was not, then, a case of rejection but a circumstantial case of discovery.

One evening he forgot to pull the plug after going to the lavatory. Later he returned to flush it.

On a shelf in the downstairs hall squatted a fat, black, heavy telephone with a big dial on the front of it. If making a trunk call, (anything other than local) those wishing to get in touch had to finger an O to get through to the exchange. During a 'trunk' call pips sounded if the talking went on for over three minutes. People often rang off very suddenly on hearing these pips as it meant they were going to have to start paying all over again. Alyson, when talking to her bed-bound cousin (after six in the evening when words cost less) nearly always cut the conversation short; mid-word. 'Bye!' she would scream as she dropped the receiver like a toasted chestnut.

To dial a number abroad it usually took ages to get through. Malise considered the idea and one afternoon, when Alyson had lumbered into the garden and everyone else seemed to be out of the way, he asked the exchange to put him through to Patricia's Lucca number.

Her bewitching voice answered 'Pronto.'

Malise shouted 'Hello. Malise. Malise Mc Hip here.' But she hung up on the instant.

Alyson had just returned, grumbling, to the hall.

'I hope you're all right dear. Has the telephone been playing up? I see you are close beside it. They say it's been affected by the weather.'

Malise glared at her, pushed past and walked out of the front door. From the gravel, beside the giant cannonball, he picked up a large, colourful pheasant's feather and walked with it, through the farmyard and past the barn where, in wintry weather, he had scrambled about with the teenage Dawn. He climbed the style and wandered into a field where he saw a large number of cowpats. Searching carefully, he decided on the biggest one in view, strode towards it and placed the feather into its middle – standing it upright. Then he returned – more or less satisfied with something but he knew not what.

There never had been a television set in the house. The wireless was the one that had entertained Christian as he listened to Just William and Monday Night at Eight O'clock – but seemed to be broken. No light relief.

With glassy eyes, he re-read Mr Scarlatti's letter and

drew a ring around the last sentence 'no one has lost what I have lost – all early hopes.' Malise found it ironic that his hopes had not even been particularly early ones.

Ruggles was stationed in the piazza beneath the high apartment for which he still paid rent but, for no reason that he understood, he did not return there. Hopes for Patricia had all but fizzled out.

With the help of the solicitor, muddled thinking from a grumpy Christian and kind neighbours, the old couple were moved into The Grid. The day before this happened, a small furniture van arrived to fetch belongings destined for the old people's home. For some unspoken reason, the old man insisted that the painting of Malise as a child was to be amongst the possessions he wished to keep with him. A hazy reminder of his wife and her final icon. As it was about to be dismantled, Malise stood before the picture in his mother's bedroom; his eyes watering. His body shook and he sobbed as he pleaded 'Patricia, for Patricia.'

'No, Malise. It's to go to The Gwid.' Christian reasoned to no avail as Malise found unexpected words.

'Mother. Mother. Patricia is your daughter. I am her father. Please understand.'

The picture, notwithstanding Malise's grovelling, was removed with resolute skill by lads in overalls.

Christian summoned the local doctor who ordered Malise a strong sedative and sent him to bed. He remained there as his childhood portrait was removed and re-hung in his father's new bedroom.

He stayed, on the doctor's advice, mildly sedated for weeks and reverted to childhood, but not childhood as he had lived it, for now he cried and uttered in a squeaky voice. He was muddled, futureless and hopelessly in love with a dream. He was a father. His boy's name was Antonio. His mother the girl with curling lips and a pink ribbon. Malise had metamorphosised into an irresponsible, wanting creature.

A single man who worked for the Air Force rented the main part of the farm house – accepting the arrangement that Malise and Christian share their own bedroom, small sitting room and kitchenette at the back.

Malise's wits went quickly – but not, exactly, by the day. Some weeks were better than others. On a good day he wandered in the garden as autumn and then winter came round – believing himself to be a rationalist and frenziedly anti-clerical.

Christian became his warden and, before long his 'memowy.'

At night the younger brother read aloud from tracts that still lay beside his bed – in honour of their late mother.

Malise sometimes interrupted fearing that he had left a spotted handkerchief in a wheelbarrow at the foot of the shrubbery.

Most days he took to walking briskly, and with his head held high as in the past, to the village shop where he bought large bunches of ripe bananas. They became speckled and slimy pretty soon. Then he would take them and bury them, using a heavy spade, to the bottom of the shrubbery near to where he had fought back, crawling about with a bushman's saw to lay the enemy low.

At times he appeared to be no more than a shapeless, speedless body of anguish.

Once only, he developed a desire to make love to

Christian as they lay on their hard beds in the dark. Neither man was young; Christian flabby in striped pyjamas. Malise yearning for any for any form of gratification.

'Would you like to try it again Christian?'

'No, thank you Malise. Never again.'

Christian was in command.

35

The old people settled at The Grid. Alyson played bridge during most hours of the day whilst her husband snoozed.

It was not the merriest of Christmases that year. Christian drove Malise to the old people's home where Alyson awaited them at the entrance.

'Daddy's not feeling very Christmassy I'm afraid. They say it's the time of year. I've ordered turkey and plum pudding but it's to be eaten cold – staff are short over the holiday.'

Malise stood stiffly and said nothing as Christian gave his stepmother an unwilling kiss.

Nobody spoke much during lunch, although Alyson and Christian did their best to disguise the silence of the others. The father was completely gaga.

By a quarter past two, the brothers had returned to their scanty quarters at the back of the house. Cold lunch had not taken long to polish off.

About six weeks later a letter came addressed to Malise.

It was opened by Christian and came from Giovanni, the one to have put Malise in touch, in the first place, with the Lucca apartment. He had, he said, written in Italian but a kind friend had translated it for him into English.

'Dear Mr Mc Hip.' In earlier days they had been on Christian name terms. 'I write to you in some distress. The apartment in Lucca that you rent from my cousin seems to have been empty for many months. No rent has been paid and several of your possessions are still there. Books, a wireless, camping equipment (including a folding tent), some samples of brickwork and a camera. Then outside, is an interesting car, an old Lagonda, which takes up space for others. Nobody knows where the key is for this car. My cousin is anxious to re-let the apartment and neighbours are getting upset about the car. The spare key to the apartment has been kept by a kind store holder in the large piazza and they had, on my cousin's instructions, let themselves in to see if your things were still there. Please can you reply to me here at the British Museum and explain this mystery.

Christian answered the letter, apologised, told of Malise's dementia and reassured Giovanni that the rent was to be paid and that he, possibly accompanied by Malise , would make plans to go to Lucca to sort things out as soon as it was possible to do so.

Malise stood, rigid and pale, and almost appealingly submissive as Christian plotted the journey. Most of the time his mind seemed to be dead blank. Sometimes it stirred and he added a comment or two.

'Yes. Lucca. Very pleasant. Bells. Many bells.'

But he was of no practical use and Christian went ahead

showing masterly power – trimming his brother's hair, shaving his face and cooking his meals. Malise was still able to scramble into his clothes and to use the lavatory where he nearly always forgot to pull the plug.

Before winter was over the brothers went together to Lucca. No key to the apartment was to be found amongst Malise's few possessions and Christian suspected him of having thrown it away in one of his rare but recurring fits of petulance. Malise was certainly in no state to travel alone and Christian enjoyed taking full charge.

In the town they met with the store holder who kept the spare key. Christian borrowed it with gratitude and the help of a dictionary. Malise almost galloped up the seventy-nine steps with glazed but shining eyes as though something tugged at him. Once there they were deafened by bells and in amongst an unmade bed, kitchen equipment and detached oddments including brick samples. Food and rubbish, it transpired, had earlier been removed by the neighbours who held the spare key. Malise stood by the window and, ape-eyed, looked at the basket attached to the rope as, Christian with unprecedented practical skill, put Malise's belongings together with the intention of wrapping and posting them during the days to come. He located the key to Ruggles under the ancient brick where it had been hidden, pocketed it and planned to decide, later, what on earth to do with the wretched car.

Malise spoke once or twice but never using more than a word at a time.

'Comestibles. Ruggles. Tent. Tent. Tent.'

Between tasks, wrapping and posting – two crates sent by sea – they ate sandwiches and drank coffee at the bar in the main piazza – the one outside which Patricia had fallen from her bike. Now they sat indoors as winter was not over. Although two of the waiters greeted him with warmth, Malise showed no signs of recognition. He just sat and, mindlessly, munched slowly on a sandwich.

One day, late in the morning, Christian ordered slices of pizza to be warmed up as Malise stared at the rails of a staircase that wound up to a sign saying 'Cabinetto.'

There was a gust, a whirlwind. Christian turned and saw a boy, no more than nine or ten years old, race towards Malise calling 'Sir. Sir. Where were you? I'll find Mamma. She's talking with her friend, at the back there. Drinking coffee.'

Having given his order, Christian returned to where Malise, unconscious of the excitement with which he had been greeted, sat. The boy had raced to retrieve his mother and was dragging her back towards the object of her mortal terror.

Patricia, clearly heavily pregnant, nodded a polite greeting towards each man. It was not long before she took stock and realised that Malise had no idea who she was; what escapades they had shared or how great had been her dread of seeing him again. All four, including the boy, were silent and confused.

Malise had mentioned to Patricia, whilst flailing in the tent, of a younger brother with a feeble temperament. No feebleness now. He took note of the size of her stomach and wondered. Dates fitted. A Mc Hip in there?

Christian smiled. Patricia, stunned and frightened, told her son that they must leave immediately. She seized his hand and whipped him towards the door as the boy nagged. 'Sir. Capitano. Why did he not know us? Who was that silly man with him? He kept laughing at his own jokes. Were they jokes?'

Faster and faster, she tugged him away, fearing her own fantasies. Had she really, less than a year ago, rolled about in a tent with that mad man? Left her son in his charge? Quite clearly he was demented. Had he been to Lucca since the tightening of the notch in his trousers? In that case she had been extremely fortunate not to have bumped into him before. Maybe his ugly brother had come especially to rescue him.

Did she hold any responsibility for the loss of his sanity?

The pizza, sizzling, was placed before the two men. Malise, still ape-eyed, asked his brother 'Who was that charming woman? Did she know me?'

It was the longest sentence he had spoken in many months but Christian found no answer to it. He was occupied in confirming dates in his head. How lucky, as it turned out, that Malise, before losing his wits, had confided in him on the topic of his love affair the previous summer. Had told of a son called 'Antonio'. It all fitted.

36

Patricia's terror of bumping into Malise in Lucca had been so fierce that she barely considered her own peculiar behaviour during the summer holiday. Aberration surely. After his letters arrived she did, at least, know that he had been crawling about in the undergrowth in Hertfordshire and tightening notches in his trousers. He had left her with no impression, though, that he might not return to Lucca at any moment.

She shuddered, trembled and her nerves quivered as she bicycled through the town wearing a black scarf and with a beret, hiding her hair, pulled well down – keeping her head as low as she dared – in terror of falling off again and of hearing his formal voice and a touch of jest saying '*Scusi signorina*. I believe we have met before.'

When off her bicycle and lying on her bed, she did begin to think back. Not for long at a time. Memories jarred her with electric shocks. Often she pulled down a shutter in her mind and made shopping lists.

A day came when she decided to stifle insupportable shame and to summon the courage to concentrate. Andrea was working in Pisa and Antonio at school for the best part of the day. She was free of duty at the art academy and decided to drive out to her house in the woods. She had shunned it since the start of term and it needed certain attentions before the winter came. Once there, it felt as if autumn had arrived. Figs lay like tiny cowpats sploshed onto the jagged terrace that surrounded the building. Wasps swarmed all over them and she was scared of being stung. They were everywhere. Buzzing around. Possibly a wasps nest in the eaves. She pulled a chair from the kitchen and placed it up against the outdoor stone table from which she looked over, across the stream, to the terrace where Malise Mc Hip had pitched his tent and where she, leaving Antonio alone in the dark wreck of a house, had pattered to indulge in reckless passion with a semi-stranger. The sudden impulse, perhaps, of a madwoman. At the same time as shaking at her memories, it did comfort her enormously to remember that she had not been entirely insane; had taken fool-proof anti-pregnancy precautions. For many years she and Andrea had hoped to have another child but, none having come along, she was fairly confident of her own infertility. Nonetheless she took no risks in that area. Huge comfort.

Then her thoughts returned to her bicycle tumble. His stately assurance. Never had she seen anyone as handsome. And English. The supper at the top of his seventy-nine steps. Had she been attracted to him then? She thought not. Not particularly. But she had enjoyed the rapport that he and her husband engaged in – although there was something stilted about the English visitor.

Later meetings. Antonio's sightseeing ventures and her boy's delicious delight in 'Sir's company.

Andrea was often working in Pisa and also often silent when at home. They did, sometimes, visit friends and relations in England but it was never a success. She did not care to dwell on that for it disappointed her. Andrea spoke reasonable English but was reluctant to do so when with her family in Essex. Her family home in Essex was not at all far from the Mc Hip farm in Hertfordshire. Might that have constituted a factor? A topographical twin-ship?

Andrea had encouraged her by saying what an interesting man she had introduced him to. He had, after all, been the one to suggest English lessons.

Maybe, during that first lunch at the *trattoria*, Malise had handed her the notion that he admired her. Apart from that, why had she behaved irrationally?

There had, to her knowledge, been no subdued hankering within her. She loved her husband, her boy and her funny little plot in the hills. Her once-weekly job at the art academy. She had a few friends from England who had settled in Lucca – taught in schools or had married Italian prisoners of war and returned with them when fighting stopped.

It was impossible for her to work out where the gaps had been in her life – or if there had been any gaps.

The Malise thing had been a blast from the blue.

She regretted it deeply. Back her mind went again as she looked to the loathsome spot on the terrace. Fireflies, candles, comestibles, strumming guitar. Maybe the wine. The admiration; flattery of a sort. Hints about being a Mc

Hip had puzzled her and had made her wonder if there had been a fashionable general or politician of that name. She took no interest in the aristocracy – had never got the hang of it.

The christening of his car 'Ruggles' had jarred slightly. An attempt at wholesome humour.

Possibly, too, he had been too successful at winning the admiration of Antonio. The understanding bachelor. The 'I might not be a father but ….'

She knew he had a slightly simple brother but had been told nothing of the scouts or the choir.

A violent attack of indigestion overpowered her. Pains near her heart. Nausea. She hoped it was indigestion and not a heart attack. She had no pills with her. Day trip. Water from the spring, cupped in her hands, gave her a break and the respite released some power with which to relive the scenes that had engulfed her only a few weeks before. Reconstructing repelled her. The sensation was entirely nasty – heart half burning and shame overpowering her. Panic of the past. Worse than the panic of the present – by far. There was sweat in her hair and round her ears as she went through inward argument. That first kiss. That had stirred something curious in her. It reminded her of something that she had missed – or thought she had missed. The past, the recent past, was a part of her and she was responsible for it. She had treated the ludicrous Englishman badly. Given encouragement.

Both her legs, from the ankles upwards, began to burn. Hot pins and needles. And her back ached. It was frightful.

Those hours (she had no idea how many) when wrapped in sex with the almost unknown visitor, haunted

her in many mysterious ways. Then her back started to itch.
Another symptom. She had nothing with her – no luggage,
no food, no alcohol. The little house was always left empty.

She cried as Antonio's voice sounded in her head
'Where is Sir? Capitano? I want him to take me on walks
again. I want him to make a camp and to drive Ruggles.
Why does he not want to be our friend anymore? *Perche
mamma?*'

The itching rose to the tops of her legs and her back
ached. Lower back. Then her right shoulder. Her memories
were killing her; suffocating her with mental shivers. Her
body underwent the mortification of having been given
away on a mattress pierced with twigs.

She threw the alabaster peach, that he had given her,
into the stream and liked hearing it plop and seeing the
water ripple. She loved the word 'plop'.

Andrea had not been able to join them for several days.
Antonio had been in a state of ecstasy. His cup was full.
Mother with him, father expected and a thrilling newcomer
with a tent and a Lagonda called 'Ruggles'. Hammock too.

During the infamy of those dizzy sexual exploits Malise
had ceased to mystify her. Whilst making love – he had
been entirely there. That was what it had boiled down to.
Total presence. Top to toe. Ecstasy. Out of doors. Crazed.
Walking back to her house on elastic steps.

He left suddenly not, he had said, wishing to be there
when her husband became part of the cast. His note. Her
relief. She had been pleased when he left. So pleased that
she had failed to suffer until later.

Some of his characteristics, in retrospect, had begun to
jar on her – such as, one evening, when he said 'I spied

some enticing herbs on the bank. Basil, rosemarina, salvia.' His words, Italianised, had made her squirm a bit. It struck her as vulgar to discuss herbs in that way. If only she had registered the absurdity of it more firmly – and retracted.

The short notes they had handed to each other in the kitchen on the day of their last meeting had been friendly and both written with the intention of continuing their affair once Antonio's holidays were over. Up the seventy-nine steps. How proud he had been of those steps.

That day, the day of Malise's departure, Andrea had found his wife much altered. She was abstracted and uninterested in his activities at the university. Antonio wanted to talk of nothing but the 'Capitano.' Why had he abandoned them after making many promises? Rides in Ruggles.

She did not write to him at the address in Lucca and did not know if he was there still.

The second day after Malise's departure was different. She flew to Andrea's side and into his arms and bed. He comforted and forgave her – not that he had more than a slight inkling that there was anything to forgive her for.

Now, later, at the scene of the crimes, she walked on tingling legs to the spot where grass was still flattened by the thin mattress and the stretch of tarpaulin. Malise had cleared up meticulously and with pride. It was as if a giant snake had left a slimy trail on the dry grass.

Her local friend came up the hill on foot carrying three letters. They spoke for a while but Patricia was clearly abstracted and her friend found her ungrateful. After all – she had been the go-between, the confidante, and expected more than an icy reception (which is what she got) after walking up the steep hill.

It was, paradoxically, the letters that cheered Patricia up and comforted her. She read them each twice as she ate only the figs not to have been invaded by wasps.

He was in the land of the living – in Hertfordshire. She realised that as she opened each letter in turn.

The first one horrified her. His description of himself crawling through the undergrowth with a bushman's saw and the cost of much blood whilst laying the enemy low, appalled her. His 'having a tale or two to tell' petrified her. As for his reference to keeping his trousers up. That disgusted her.

The second and the third letters were all in the same vein but each one reminded her of the notch in his belt.

She walked to the village shop where she bought paper and an envelope. A letter could be posted on her way home.

At the stone table she wrote the cruel letter that triggered off the reply (received some weeks later) of 'Whoa there!'

She had always abhorred screech marks and his letters screeched with them. Poor Malise. The letters he had troubled himself with had been a part of his undoing.

Again and again, the closeness that had sprung up out of nothing and ended quickly, plunged her into misery. She had not wanted to enter his world but he had, inexorably, entered hers.

After writing the letter, she walked into the house. It was dark and damp but very pretty – trees almost breaking in through the windows, she opened the one in her bedroom and heard birds twitter as wasps buzzed. She was thankful

that she had never shared that room with Mc Hip. Maybe
out of doors didn't count. The house was not contaminated.
That was a blessing. Winter wind and rain might dispose of
outside evidence. She spotted the pink ribbon that had tied
her hair back on the day of Malise's arrival at La Cassetta. It
lay on a table beside her bed. The double bed she shared
with Andrea. She walked down the chipped, stone stairs to
the kitchen where she found a pair of scissors and cut the
ribbon into tiny shreds. Malise became no more, in her
identity, than a blunt instrument. A garden tool. The
memory of his tool provoked an unsteady reaction and she
sat down again. One more walk past the oozing, open-
mouthed, wasp-infected figs and onto a raised patch of grass
where the two trees, between which the hammock had been
hitched, leant towards each other – faintly scarred where
knots had been tied around their trunks.

She tore up his letters and shoved them into a plastic
bag alongside her shredded ribbon.

The magic of the place began to return in shafts of
light. The grizzly episode had, after all, lasted but a few
days. Even by magnifying those days by five, or even fifty,
recovery was not going to last forever.

She had driven back to Lucca, clutching her
discreditable secret, where she fetched Antonio from
school.

Her terror of meeting Malise, were he to return from
England, lasted for several months and then disappeared
altogether. It was as if he had never been. She did not
know, though, that he, too, was becoming as if he had
never been.

Later in the year, as winter arrived, she sat with Andrea

at the stone table. Both wore overcoats. Then she said to him 'Andrea. We are to become parents again.' Andrea was more than amazed and overjoyed. Ecstatic. Proud and dazed. He told her how happy he had been during their few last days together during the summer holiday.

'What, I wonder,' he asked as he drank coffee and smoked 'became of that strange Englishman? Malise Mc Hip. The one we met in Lucca and who spent a few nights here in his tent.'

Patricia quaked as he went on 'We are, I think, lucky to be rid of him. He was interesting and educated but I didn't care for the way he worked in order to impress Antonio. It was a little suspicious – as if he wanted to give us lessons in parenting.'

She answered, 'He was an oddity. I liked him to start with, then, well to tell you the truth, I went right off him.'

She looked at her happy husband with dedication. He was an excellent person. How could she have been unfaithful to him? As she wondered about that, she realised that she had never, ever been unfaithful. She had strayed, to be sure, but had never stopped loving Andrea. The realisation cheered her up. 'He was odd; fishy. Handsome to an eerie degree. Snobbish. Self-righteous. Conceited.' Patricia began to revel in her own and her husband's opinion of the strange man who had not hesitated to seduce her.

Various things had to be dealt with before the damp became damper. Logs to be stacked in the shed. Logs that had been left behind by the gypsies who Malise, from his hammock, had thought of tackling on Patricia's behalf as they walked away with large bundles.

37

Several months later Christian sent Ruggles's ignition key to Patricia. Registered. Malise sat silent and uninterested as his brother wrote the letter to accompany it. Christian had read Patricia's letter of dismissal and, with Malise's earlier confessions on his mind, felt, in his limited way, that he understood a little of what had taken place.

'Here comes the key to my brother's Lagonda. I am sure that he would like to remind you that he always called it 'Ruggles'. I have never known why he chose that name. The car is still parked (here he gave the particulars) and ready for your collection. I have power of attorney and am happy on his behalf to give you the car as a present to your unborn child in memory of my brother. I have reason to believe that I may well be the child's uncle.'

Christian sat quietly after writing the letter and fantasised that, one day, he might turn up in Lucca to claim the child. The last of his particular branch of Mc Hips. He, after all, with Malise's wits gone, was the head of the family and had rights.

Patricia, within weeks of giving birth to her second child, found the hard packet – key and letter within, on her door mat. Feeling clammy and hysterical she called a mechanic and asked him to join her beside Ruggles. Fortunately Antonio had never known that the car remained in Lucca and had asked no questions as to its whereabouts. The mechanic, with difficulty, managed to get Ruggles's engine running. At that point Patricia asked him if the car might be of any use to him. He was welcome to own it. The young man, mystified, accepted the offer and drove away in it. He sold it almost at once. It went to a buyer in Florence so was, no more, to be seen on the streets in or around the city of Lucca.

38

After some negotiations, one of the rooms at the farm house was reclaimed from the tenant. He was a nice but pernickety man and insisted on a reduced rent. Christian needed the extra room for he could no longer look after his brother single-handedly and a live-in helper was needed.

Malise had become irrational – buying more and more bananas; removing paintings from the walls, carrying them clumsily to the barn where he stacked them beside the spot, now sacred, on which, in his youth, he had rolled in the straw with Dawn.

Sometimes he disappeared altogether and had to be tracked down by the local policeman.

A live-in helper was finally found. Her name was Kathleen and, to begin with, Malise fell for her. She was sixty two years old and had been through rough patches in her life.

It had not been easy for Christian to persuade anyone to take the job. Two bachelors, one of them mad and both creepy, living in isolation, did not attract many candidates.

On the first day he was wary but on the second, Malise ran his hands over her face and mumbled the name 'Patricia' through half-closed lips.

'No dear. Kathleen. Not Patricia.'

That made him cross.

'I call you Patricia. Trish. Pat. Tricia. Pat. Trish.'

'Very well. Call me names. I am called Kathleen all the same.'

She liked the running of his hands over her face but when they descended to her body she felt compelled to object.

'No dear. Nothing naughty.'

For the first few weeks he went quietly and enjoyed her attention. He followed her around wherever she went and continued to call her Patricia. Trish. Pat. Tricia or whatever related shortening came into his head.

Christian steered clear of them both and returned to his duties. Choir and Boy Scouts.

After some months, though, when it was clear that Kathleen was going to continue to reject any sexual advances, Malise began to get violent. One of his father's old walking sticks stood in a holder by the back door. He brandished it and brought it down on her shoulder leaving her with a nasty bruise.

When Christian returned from a choir meeting he was met by a bedraggled Kathleen who insisted on showing him black marks on her shoulder.

At first she had wanted to call the police but caution told her to control her instinct. She was not well paid but it was at least, a job and she did not lose touch with the fact that Christian was, after all, a bachelor. Malise was very handsome – if violent and abusive. But she could no longer manage him on her own. He started throwing things at her, kitchen utensils, china and tins of food, as he shouted 'Patricia' at concert pitch. Then he was up half the night unhooking pictures from the walls – ready to remove to the barn when day broke.

The kitchen had to be declared out of bounds after an unnerving incident. Consequently it became the place where Malise most wanted to be.

The unnerving incident took place as Kathleen watched an early evening programme on a newly installed black and white television set. Malise had wandered into the kitchen where a fearsome animation overtook him and he pulled a large pudding basin from a sagging shelf. Then he investigated the store cupboard. Methodically but with shaky hands, he collected together an assortment of food stuffs and emptied samples into the bowl. First a can of brightly coloured soup, then corn flakes, chocolate powder – stiff and stinking with mouse droppings, condensed milk, golden syrup, marmite, and crumbled digestive biscuits. All he could lay his trembling hands on. After a while the bowl was full and the mixture slopped over its sides. Malise stirred awkwardly with a wooden spoon and spoke (to himself) 'Patricia. Patricia is coming to supper. Up seventy-nine steps.' He said that in his head over and over again. Then, drawing himself tall, he took the bowl and its swilling contents and hurled it at the window – cracking the glass and leaving trails of glutinous slime over table, sink and window sill.

Christian was adamant that he could not afford another

pair of hands. His brother would have to go into a home of sorts.

Malise did nothing but try to batter down the door leading to the kitchen.

New arrangements took time to sort out and caused much anxiety but were finally arrived at. Malise went but Kathleen refused to do so. She now had her eye firmly on Christian and, after a prolonged and difficult courtship, caught him and forced him to the altar. He was involved in the local church and refused to have the marriage conducted anywhere but there. Using a ring once worn by Christian's devout late mother, he made promises to the older woman – never for an instant suspecting that the union was bigamous.

The pair rather enjoyed each other's company and alternated between visiting the very old couple at The Grid and Malise at the nearby home for those suffering from conditions of the mind.

Christian and Kathleen bought a dog and, for the first year of their non-consummated and illegal marriage, when not visiting the old or the mad, enjoyed walking Patricia, as the dog was called (they both felt that the absent Patricia had brought them together) and bringing back belongings from the barn where Malise had built a shrine to the memory of his youthful pleasures.

39

The old father and Alyson died within three weeks of each other and Kathleen much enjoyed the power of being in charge of funeral arrangements and of reclaiming objects from the Grid – including the portrait of Malise as a beautiful child. She had hoped that there might be a stirring of interest among aristocratic relations after she paid to have a notification of the funeral printed in *The Times* newspaper but none, if there were any left, showed interest.

Christian was now in charge of all family money and, before long, he and Kathleen gave notice to the nice RAF tenant and took over the old rooms. Christian was insistent that they move back into his childhood bedroom and that Kathleen should occupy the bed once slept in by Malise. No mention was made of the activities that took place on the floor of that room during the brothers' early years.

At the nearby home for demented patients, Malise lingered on, doped and querulous, never uttering more than the word 'Patricia'. His hair went white and his eyes watered constantly. He was not old and still remarkably handsome, although his back teeth showed decay, and liked to look at himself in the vast, gold-framed glass that hung outside his cubicle door.

One evening, as Christian and Kathleen, ate toasted cheese in the kitchen (once banned to Malise) Christian suddenly said 'He must be fwee by now'.

'Free? Oh dear no. They'll never let him out. Not in his condition.'

'Fwee. Fwee years old. The child.'

'Oh no. Not that dear. Don't even think about it.'

The last thing Kathleen wanted was a little Mc Hip to gather what would, eventually, be left. Christian, although younger by far than her, might expire first and leave her in full charge of everything – Malise's portrait included.

'It would be interwesting to find out.'

'No dear. We've nothing to go on and to let sleeping dogs lie is always the best policy.'

The subject was dropped for a while but Christian continued to brood.

Visits to Malise had to be paid – not that the visitors or the visited gained any pleasure from them. On one occasion Christian, in a hearty mood, addressed his brother who sat, sedated and goofy, in a dirty armchair.

'So Malise. How are they tweating you?'

No reply. Not even a tweet.

Kathleen chipped in 'they say this is a nice place Malise. Of course we wish you were back with us at the farm but we are happy there and never forget that you now have me as a sister.'

No reply.

Christian always had a book of jokes and riddles by him. He sifted through the book after looking at his Half Hunter watch – once the property of Malise but now appropriated, and said, 'Midday Malise. Talking of time, did you know what the Leaning tower of Pisa said to Big Ben?'

A mention of Pisa, near to Lucca after all, might spark something off in the poor, lapsed memory.

No reply.

'If you've got the time I've got the inclination.' He doubled with loud laughter as the pair made their getaway.

40

'As you know dear, I'm happy to see to bits and bobs for you.' Kathleen's teeth were enormous and her hair very dark excepting the roots.

She was content to be running the house and felt more or less safe from her past. No one, now that she had become a Mc Hip, was likely to track her down. Her troublesome 'first' husband had, she had learnt many years before, also indulged in a bigamous marriage so was unlikely to wish to upset any apple carts.

'Yes Kathleen. You are a gweat help here.'

'It's Malise and that dentist that are bothering me.'

'What dentist is that?'

'The one who visits patients at the Olive Branch. Where they look after your brother.' She added the last words in case he had forgotten what The Olive Branch was, for Christian, too, was becoming forgetful.

'What has a dentist to do with it?'

'There's one, a foreigner, I don't like to call him a darkie, who does the rounds there. He inspects the teeth of dwellers; patients I should say. Matron wanted a word with me when I went on Saturday.'

'What did she say?'

'It seems that the dentist thinks money ought to be spent on his back teeth. The front ones are doing all the chewing. He says bacteria may form and cause cancer. Scaremongering I call it.'

'We'd better go ahead. I'll pay with Malise's money and he's still got stacks.'

'How shall I put it? Is it worth it? They say he won't last forever you know.'

Christian made no reply.

Kathleen, slightly tipsy, enlarged on the topic of unnecessary extravagance. She wasn't exactly drunk but had arrived at the stage when she knew, if she took another sip, she was certain to be. She took another sip and was.

'Christian. When I consented to be your wife, I expected a little more from you. Our bedroom, for a start. Does it hold some guilty secret? Why can't we move ourselves into more comfortable quarters? Why not the large room with the pretty curtains?'

Christian was dumb as she filled her glass with more wine.

'Then, when it comes to Malise's money. You have power of attorney. Why can't we help ourselves and have the larger bedroom done over?'

No longer dumb, Christian answered 'I shall use Malise's money to go in search of his child. There may yet be Mc Hips living here one day.'

41

The odd couple scoured an attic where, in a cedar wood chest, Christian found an old coat, possibly once worn by his grandfather. It was long and dark – the darkness tinged with green from age; made of Melton cloth and with a squirrel lining. It had long deep pockets and, having been packed in moth balls, had survived well.

Kathleen was pleased too. She unearthed an Astrakhan coat, once the property of Alyson, and sent it to the cleaners. The lining to one of the pockets was ripped but she clipped the two torn bits together with safety pins. They took a slow train to Dover. It was cold and smoky but Kathleen rejoiced that the money for Malise's back teeth had at least been spent on a trip. Not that she approved of the trip either but considered it preferable to Malise's back teeth. She was bored rigid by visiting her brother-in-law in his demented state and by sharing that grim room with Christian and his warped but unspoken memories of childhood. She had been happy, though, to find a wad of *lires* in a drawer, left over from Malise's emotionally charged visit to Italy.

The crossing was rough and Kathleen, a poor sailor, vomited as Christian showed his true boy scout spirit and watched the White cliffs fade from sight. Between violent bouts of retching, she asked 'Didn't you once tell me that you used to have a pen friend in France? Something to do with the Scouts?'

'I did but Malise said it was babyish and tore the letters up. I let it go after that.'

It was a struggle – getting off the boat and getting onto the train bound for Paris. Cigarette fumes changed from Craven A to Gauloise. Kathleen had been to Paris before but denied it when speaking to Christian for fear of revealing anything connected with her past. She was glad of the Astrakhan coat, although it was rather heavy and one of the ripped pockets still contained an old shopping list left over from one of Alyson and Christian's outings to the Coop.

They spent a terrible night on the train from Paris to Pisa. Their couchette compartment was designed for six horizontal travellers and the slats on which they slept were made up of dark green, formica. Very slippery. The four slats not occupied by Christian and Kathleen were taken over by loud, male students who smoked and spoke all through the night. It was early when the train passed through a customs check. Much shouting of '*Dogana*' but nobody came near them. Kathleen was relieved for fear of carrying too much contraband cash. Later, at a station, men with packed breakfasts in pink paper boxes strolled the platform yelling 'Café, *panini, banani*,' and the night was over.

42

They caught a train that went slowly from Pisa to Lucca. The wooden slats on which they perched bulged with darkly dressed Italians and were uncomfortable. Christian read, many times, from the notebook that he carried in his coat pocket. In the book was written the name and address of Patricia, her husband and, in all probability, her two children. His uncertain mission was in progress and he looked committed as he heaved their suitcases down from a meshed rack above his head at Lucca station which, in spite of the efforts of Mussolini, was dark and cheerless. There they asked a loitering fellow passenger to direct them to a *pensione*. '*Costo Poco*' he said several times and very adamantly.

They walked, dragging cases, one containing Christian's Teddy Bear, to the *pensione* that almost touched the station building. A furious man at a desk asked for immediate payment before pointing, grumpily, at a flight of filthy stairs. Their room was musty. It stank of cigarettes and the terrazzo floor, patterned as an ailing liver, was stained and chipped. There was a high, small window a low hard bed and a bumpy pillow apiece. No food on offer there. Nobody spoke English nor did Christian and Kathleen speak any Italian. It was mid morning but after a night with no sleep, Christian's intentions were still firm – even if he barely knew what they amounted to.

'We'll play it by ear,' he said as they sat in misery in the dark, damp room. He suddenly itched for a boy scout. A small boy called Joey. Christian remembered Joey's bright smile that had exhilarated him at one of his lowest moments – soon after Malise left home for boarding school.

Although the *pensione* stood outside the Lucca walls, only a short walk was needed, through one of the historic gateways, to reach the city centre.

He was compelled to make his way, Kathleen puffing beside him in her astrakhan coat, to the Piazza San Michele and the bar where he had, with a demented Malise, encountered the pregnant Patricia where she carried, quite possibly, an embryonic Mc Hip.

At first they stood in the bar. No seats were free. Christian asked for two slices of pizza and a strong drink for both of them. They perched on stools beside the busy bar. He watched Kathleen dig her enormous teeth into her pizza slice and winced as melted cheese oozed out between them. Seats became free and the pair moved into a dark corner of the café. Kathleen faced him. She dreaded returning to the horrible *pensione* and had no strength with which to peruse the town.

'So, Christian. Why, exactly, are we here?'

'Mission dear. I wish to know if I have a little nephew or niece in this town.'

'But would they be dear? Even if ....' She stared at him with ferocity.

'Well. Blood is blood Kathleen and we are, er, well, you know ....'

'What do I know? Nothing of your relatives apart from the old ones who have gone and Malise who wouldn't make much of a daddy. If you remember not one of them responded to my funeral notice in *The Times* and that was not cheap to insert.'

He ignored the reference to his dismissive cousins and said 'Well. Daddy – no – but blood is what counts.'

'Even so dear.' More cheese oozed as she signalled to a waiter to bring her a glass of brandy – shortage of funds or not. 'Are you intending to call on these people? The Leris? What will you say to them? The husband for one, might object and the wife might deny any knowledge of your brother.'

'The boy. Her son. He will wemember. He did when we met up with them on this vewy spot.'

'What if it breaks the family up?'

'Can't be helped. The child would have the wight to know of his or her blood line. Mc Hip.'

The brandy arrived. She drank it fast and ordered another.

Christian became melancholy. 'We should have discussed this more fully before we came I know, but here we are and, yes. We will call on them this evening. Why not? Nothing to lose.'

'Plenty for them to lose if you go telling the husband

about his wife's fling with Malise. He may never have heard of it. What's more – what on earth do you intend to do with this three year old if you note a family resemblance? I'm not looking after it and that's for sure.'

The second brandy was taking effect and she ordered a third.

Christian left her to drink and went away hoping to buy a map of the city.

When he returned to join her it was obvious that there was no question of calling on anyone that day. Kathleen was drowsy, hiccoughing, and barely able to rise from the table. The bill was unnervingly large. They walked, very unsteadily, to the horrible *pensione* and flopped onto the hard, low bed. In the passage there was a lavatory and basin. No bath. The cistern of the lavatory was broken and the top lay in dirty fragments on the wet floor. Water in the cistern was bright orange with rust. No paper and no water from the single tap above the cracked basin. Kathleen retched and semi-sobbed before slumping beside Christian. They both stayed there, getting very thirsty, until the following day.

No food was available in that dark place so, when they were dressed but still unwashed, they trotted once again into the town in search of coffee and a croissant. The Astrakhan coat fell heavily on Kathleen's shoulders and her head ached appallingly and they trudged back to the bar of the day before.

43

After drinking coffee, they faced each other once again.

'So. Christian. Are we going to call on those poor Leris today?'

'That's the idea.'

'It's a bad one. I'm not going with you.'

'As you please.'

'It isn't that I'm pleased by any of it. The horrible hotel. It's cold and filthy. Let's go home.'

'Not yet Kathleen.'

'Then you go your way and I'll go mine. We'll meet at that dreadful place this evening before going out to eat.'

'As you say, Pwobably better that way,'

The squirrel lined coat was too hot and heavy for the time of year. Harsh winter had not arrived and that particular November was a mild one – if damp. Christian sweated but walked briskly – comparing map with address book – to a less populated part of the city but within its walls. The map and the note book guided him to a front door. It appeared to belong to a ground floor apartment that stood on a quiet and pleasant street. Brickwork galore. He remembered brickwork from having listened to many of Malise's verbal rambles. He rang the bell and heard it shrill. It was answered, almost at once, and there, in front of him, stood the undeniably beautiful Patricia. She knew, immediately, that calamity, under a squirrel lined coat, had struck. Christian was a rough and distorted version of Malise and she remembered him well from their hideous encounter when Malise had, thanks to heaven, failed to recognise her or her son, Antonio. She had been pregnant at that time and had noted, with horror, Christian's interested eyes dwelling upon her swollen stomach.

A weird chill settled on her forehead. Her breath came in sharp pants.

'Come in. Can I help you? My husband is upstairs and the children are both out with their grandmother. She always takes them out on a Sunday. I was painting and must return to work very soon. Just tell me what I can do for you.' She heard her voice coming from another corner of the room and wondered why she had told him that her mother in law always took the children out on Sundays. She had not wished to tell him anything at all. Her mind was disordered and she wondered if she was dreaming or, shockingly, awakening. She shouted to Andrea. 'Come at once.'

Christian followed her into a pretty sitting room – much influenced in style by Patricia's informal English taste. Cushions, pictures, rugs and comforts. There they stood. Andrea joined them. He had never seen this oddly attired stranger but something in his flavour gave a hint. It reminded him of the Englishman, Malise Mc Hip, who had entered and departed from their lives at equal speed.

'How do you do?' Andrea held out his hand to Christian.

'Are you visiting our beautiful city? You have, perhaps, an introduction to us through mutual friends?'

'Not pwecisely. My bwother knew you I believe. Malise Mc Hip.'

Patricia sat down and her temperature rose. How dare they? One brief, shabby episode in her happy life had returned to cause her anguish. Was there no such thing as the forgotten past?

Andrea continued. 'Your brother. We knew him very slightly for a very short time. We are busy people and cannot entertain you but, if you need, I will give you advice of where eating is good in Lucca. Now we must both return to our work before my mother returns with our two children.'

'Two'. Christian was resolute. 'It's the young one I want to meet. There might be an – er – connection.'

This was more than the baffled couple were able to take.

Andrea said 'I'll show you his photograph and then you must go.' His voice was tense and angry. He picked a framed photograph of a child with clear cut features and crisp dark hair. He handed it to Christian. 'That is Ezra. He has a typical and fine Jewish face. See his long flexible hands. We named him after his grandfather who he resembles closely.'

Patricia held her head in her hands and trembled. Horror shot through her and her eyes watered. She understood what this creature was driving at and knew him to be semi insane but, nonetheless, he brought shame and debilitation.

Andrea took back the photograph and almost shovelled Christian to the front door. The heavily coated fellow had no desire for more. Whether or not he would, left to himself, have recognised the child as being, most definitely, not a Mc Hip, he was unsure but he knew that there was no future in his quest.

Andrea and Patricia were left to steady themselves and return to yet a fuller understanding of each other.

44

Malise, imprisoned at the Olive Branch, was unaware of almost everything although he still took pleasure in guzzling food. A sense of dumb trouble showed in his eyes but, in more lucid moments, he continued to feed recklessly on illusions – sobbing and calling out Patricia's name as he counted steps. He was, by a long way, the youngest patient in the care home – and medical advisors were mystified upon learning that dementia had set in at such an early age.

Christian had been asked, at the start, whether Malise had suffered external stress of any kind – had he had an extreme reaction to rejection for instance?

'I vewwy much doubt it' he had replied.

Malise's nocturnal confessions whilst sharing a room with his brother had held no real importance for Christian. He had enjoyed the position of superiority that accompanied them but had little understanding of the true cause of Malise's anguish, even if, later, he decided to put the disclosures to (what he considered to be) good use.

Different doctors had suggested different diagnoses. Nobody arrived at conclusions – other than to agree that the condition stemmed from nothing but extraordinarily and very unusual bad luck as the result of having been dealt some emotional shock.

Nina, one of the nurses, particularly enjoyed caring for Malise. His hands did not wander over her, as they had done in the case of Kathleen, for his limbs were cold and almost lifeless. Nina liked to gaze at him. 'If only I could, I'd have his teeth fixed, then I'd frame him and hang him on the wall in a lovely gold frame,' she'd tell her friend. 'Fancy anyone as handsome as that losing their wits so young. If I'd been him I'd have glanced in the mirror once a day and cheered myself up.'

'Handsome is as handsome does' her friend answered – although she had no understanding whatsoever of what the saying told her.